PRACTICAL
BLASPHEMY

—

THE NEW TESTAMENT

LJT

ANTIBOOKCLUB

NEW YORK

Published in 2019 by ANTIBOOKCLUB

Design by Najeebah Al-Ghadban

ISBN 9780997592313 (paperback)

Library of Congress Control Number: 2019940401

Published in the United States of America

10 9 8 7 6 1 2 3 4 5

PRACTICAL
BLASPHEMY

1. Clean the house
   - mirrors and windows
   - vacuum and mop
   - dishes
   - fold laundry
   - bring in garbage cans

2. Stock refrigerator
   - green beans
   - coffee
   - soy milk
   * make fresh sweet tea
   -pork loin
   - corn
   - peanut butter
   - granola bars
   - dog treats
   - laundry detergent

3. Goodwill
   - drop off clothes and shoes

4. Goodbyes
   - call family and say "I love you"
   - take Blue to the dog park
   (with special treats)
   - mail letters

5. Smoke the biggest joint you can roll

6. Play the Rachmaninoff Prelude in C♯ minor

7. Drink a cup of Earl Grey tea

8. Shave head (?)

9. Put Blue in the bedroom with his favorite pillow and squirrel toy

10. DIE DIE DIE DIE DIE DIE DIE DIE DIE DIE DIE DIE DIE DIE DIE DIE
    DIE DIE DIE DIE DIE DIE DIE DIE DIE DIE DIE DIE DIE DIE DIE DIE
    DIE DIE DIE DIE DIE DIE DIE DIE DIE DIE DIE DIE DIE DIE DIE DIE
    DIE DIE DIE DIE DIE DIE DIE DIE DIE DIE DIE DIE DIE DIE DIE DIE
    DIE DIE DIE DIE DIE DIE DIE DIE DIE DIE DIE DIE DIE DIE DIE DIE
    DIE DIE DIE DIE DIE DIE DIE DIE DIE DIE DIE DIE DIE DIE.

PART I

REVELATION

I want to cut off my eyelids. Amelia folds the to-do list neatly in half, and chastises her own thoughts. Hush. This is supposed to be a day of gratitude. She pushes the image from her mind *slice the eyelids* and focuses on the promise of her impending death. Freedom. Independence Day. Flashes of flags and balloons, somehow always red, white, and blue balloons · · ·They choke the sea turtles. Miles Davis's "Bitches Brew" screaming through her mind. Creeping. Uninvited. Can't have that. I'm not going out like that. Her continuous musical hallucinations plague her like Miles's stringent timbre needles the brain. She is prepared.

The brilliant play of early afternoon light on the CD labeled DEATH MIX in her hand is two-dimensional and colorless to her. Couldn't think of anything more subtle? Amelia talked about suicide so often that her friends didn't blink an eye when she included it in the rotation about a month ago. Just another interesting quirk. Just another dark joke. After I'm dead, they'll call this a "red flag."

The stereo opens. She carefully slides the disc into place and pushes the play button. Debussy. The prelude to "Suite Bergamasque" **F major** · · · A warm key · · · Rubato. The octaves boom over each other and settle into the space under her collarbones, broadening her. She thinks about all the time she spent finding the perfect version for this moment. So many pianists mangle it. She agrees with herself · · · They rush it. They don't let it into their marrow. Impressionism. Monet. Manet. Art Institute. Free Student Tuesdays. Chicago skyline. Her fingers twitch. Maybe I should play it. I have time to play it. But today is a day of gratitude · · · Not regret. Amelia is grateful to herself that she has chosen the perfect music to accompany her into the dark. The Richter interpretation is the best.

Amelia takes off her clothes unceremoniously and stuffs them down the trash chute. The music rings in the vaulted ceiling of her skylight bathroom as she slides open the glass door. The grout around the deep Jacuzzi tub is shoddy and Amelia can feel the jagged edges in the back of her throat. She ignores the mirror and the voice in her head · · · *Fatty fatty fat fat, gonna kill herself naked in the tub like a stuck pig squealing for death* · · · Part of her wants to count her ribs and slit her wrists on her hip bones, but she doesn't want Mirror Amelia to reach through the glass. Mirror Amelia is vicious. Mirror Amelia started moving independently a few months ago, so she only washes half of her face at a time, always keeping an eye on the phantom. Amelia repeats herself. Today is a day of gratitude ::SNEER::

They are all excited. Out of the infinite voices and facets of personality she has in her head, every single one is in favor of this decision. Finally, something on which we all agree. I hate them. I wish I could cut them out of my brain. Fry them out. Sting them out · · · Hold in the doctor's hands the wasps of healing and let them sting me to death. The song changes. Kurt, I'm sorry. Janis. Elliott. Sarah Kane—who was surprised when she killed herself? Every one of her plays encased in despair. Jimi Hendrix. Jeff Buckley. Jim Morrison. We KNEW, and we let them all die anyway. She sees the bemused faces of her friends on her mind-screen. I wonder how long they waited. I wonder how long they waited to die as I have waited. *Gouges in the eyes* · · · *Hurt the eyes* · · · Stop it! Can we all just focus here? You're spending your last hour thinking about crushing your eyeballs? What the fuck, man? Today is a day of . . . ? *GRATITUDE!* chirp the perpetually excited kindergarteners. That's better. Her eyes soften and she allows a slight smile.

In her mind's eye, a crow stands watch over an old box cutter on the side of the empty tub beneath the skylight. She looks, tearing her eyes away from the mirror. Like a monk, she repeats her mantra. Today is a day of gratitude. Escape. I'll be rid of that terror once and for all. Disembodied hands disembodied Cheshire cat smile *Alice in Wonderland* THE MIRROR. The music becomes delicate, distracting her. Amelia does not turn on the water, but steps into the dry bathtub naked. Less dramatic. The kindergarteners are afraid that insects will come swarming out of the jets. For ten years my head has been crawling with cockroaches. So what if they did swarm? she allays the fear. Wouldn't that be appropriate? She has waited a decade to silence the sadists the pushovers the children the typing hands the part of her that is John Wayne Gacy the part of her that is Mother Teresa. It all must end.

Let me peel off your skin for you, Honey. We can make beef jerky earrings or something sad that smells like blood. Let me use you · · · Suck out your eyeballs · · · Rape you with a barbeque fork. Show you the ruins of your soul so you can thank God that there is no such thing.

She has been praying for nearly ten years. Praying for God to save her from her own untrustworthy brain, from being tortured by demons and fallen angels. She has been praying for the voices to stop, for the music to be silenced, for the nightmares and suicidal obsessions to end. What a coward. Mother Mary's statue crying bloody tears, It's rigged! The Pope posing with *Piss Christ*.

Waiting hasn't worked. Praying hasn't worked. It's time to take personal responsibility and end it myself.

Like any musician, Amelia obsesses over timing. *Do it,* her consciousness speaks first. Do it. *Do it,* they add. *Do it!* Do it. *Do it!* chorus the kindergarteners. *Do it,* type the disembodied hands. Her thoughts frantic, urging her on. *It's time.* She holds the blade to her upper forearm, takes a deep breath, and slices down to her wrist · · · *cracking ice crows flying from a white tree the dark is rising* · · · an explosion of thought and sensation. She opens her eyes to assess the damage.

The gash is four inches long and barely a quarter-inch deep ::LAUGHTER:: Are you fucking kidding me? She can see the fat beneath the skin as the wound wells with blood. She makes another incision to the arm with the dull blade. The crow throws its head back and caws. *Goddamnit!* In a fit of rage, she hacks into her left arm, creating a bloody mess. The fascia under the skin suddenly bulges out. She panics at the sight of it. Breathe. Breathe. Your skin is an organ and it holds you all in. Nothing to fear, let it out. Listen to the music. Elliott stabbed himself in the heart, twice. *STAB STAB STAB* in the chest his chest her chest yes, yes, I'm ready to die. The right arm is easier because now she knows what to expect from the blade. She thinks of all the movie suicides she's ever seen; the lame tearing-paper sound and clever camera cutaways play in rapid succession behind her corneas ::SCHICKSCHICKSCHICK:: People would think differently about it if they knew how gross it looks. It's much more difficult when you're using your nondominant hand, slippery with blood.

Amelia studies her wounds, running red, decides they're sufficient to kill her. Not pretty, but it should do. She relaxes in the empty bathtub, looking up through the skylight, the corners of her mouth turned toward her ears. Everyone is satisfied. Every voice and perspective in her head goes mute. Only music. I'm sorry we abandoned you, she thinks to Elliott. I'm sorry you suffered for no reason. And I understand. You escaped. I will escape, too. The drums enter as her thoughts wander.

Is not from the mouth of the Most High that good AND bad come? Why should any who draw breath complain about the punishment of their sins?

Her blood feels silky against her skin. The serpent slithers into her.

Eeeeeeeeevvvve, it whispers. *Will you pick me up and ssset me in that heavy branchsssh there, by your ear?*

Amelia nods, gently picking up the serpent. God flicks the serpent's forked tongue out of its mouth for want of her skin, for the taste of her, and she notices.

The serpent-God slithers, wraps itself around a delectable piece of fruit and hisses, *Becaussse you have helped me, I shhhhhall give you a reward. What would you like, mossst of all?*

"I want nothing more than to taste the fruit around which you are coiled and be spared from its poison."

The serpent flicks out its tongue and shudders, dislodging the fruit which falls neatly into her smooth pink palm.

I ssssswear to you, if you eat thisss fruit, no harm shhhhhall come of it, vows the serpent-God.

Amelia takes a cautious bite of the ripe flesh, bursting with gratitude. The room distorts.

FINALLY.

She gropes for her phone and clumsily dials 911.

A bored voice answers. "911. Is this an emergency?"

"No."

"Please hold."

Metallica rings in the silence.

A different woman picks up the line. "911, how can I help you?"

Amelia leans back, cross-legged in the tile tomb, "I'm about to die, and I want you to come pick up my body."

"What?"

"I'm committing suicide and I want you to come pick up my body so my roommate doesn't have to find it." Twenty minutes.

"Where are you located?"

"115 Montrose, apartment C. Please specify that they are not to use any sirens or make a scene."

"Don't do it! You have so much to live for—"

Amelia throws her phone against the wall and it shatters. She closes her eyes and waits for her song to finish. To die.

Finally.

Her agony bounces from darkness to light, sometimes colliding with thoughts. No resonating or deeply affective last words. Brickles—that electronic blip on the screen that is my sorrow ::PLINKPLINK:: It catches between the top and the bottom and erases her, wipes away what is constant and leaves only blackness and an environment. Edges soften until she's staring at the screen of herself. DE TACHE D. *Take out the eyes.* That was my favorite sound · · · the erasing part, like winning in skeeball *eat the umbilical cord* until it was replaced by the THX test sound in movie theaters. I feel more whole listening to that than Mozart. *Bleed the stuck pig.* THAT is the failure of mankind. The voices go silent. She listens to James Hetfield beg for forgiveness.

And then there are sirens.

Amelia panics. A horse whinnies in her head, as clear as the voices of the men downstairs, then her musical hallucinations return

6

in full force. The heavy door at the stairwell outside the building is locked with a thick deadbolt. The Avalanches blast through her mind. Response time is twenty minutes! It was supposed to be twenty minutes!

The men break through the lobby door. She grabs the box cutter and slashes her inner elbows open as Blue barks and scratches desperately at the door in his room. EMTs bang on the apartment door as another horse whinnies · · · "Frontier Psychiatrist." The voices chorus in her head. The volume is unbearable. The EMTs break down the door.

"GET OUT!" she screams from the bathroom. "Get the fuck out and just let me die!"

She wrestles against them, a bloody, naked savage.

"We're here to help."

"Where are your clothes?"

Amelia fights them, screaming, as they drag her slippery form out of the tub and try to subdue her. "I don't have any clothes," she snarls. "I threw them away, you FUCK, get the FUCK OUT OF MY HOUSE!" The horse whinnies again as the choir *ohs* and *ahs*. "I told you no sirens! I told you not to make a scene!" A record player scratches over voices in her head in the places where she doesn't know the lyrics. Blue is slamming his body against the bedroom door, trying to get to her. *Slash murder die die.* She wills herself to bleed to death, fights harder knowing her heart rate is rising.

They wrap Amelia in a blanket pulled from the couch and carry her downstairs while she laughs and cries and screams all at the same time, the music pounding in her skull. As they rush her into the ambulance, the string quartet begins. Amelia only glimpses them, but she can see that people are gathered around and staring. The doors of the ambulance slam shut. *Boom-kak!* Faces asking her questions, bodies holding her down. The paramedic's face a yellow plastic Lego head.

"You did the right thing in calling us. You're gonna be okay. Everything is gonna be okay." He surveys her mangled forearms. "Where the hell are we gonna put the IV?"

"Hand!" answers an astronaut. They place the needle in her pinned arm. She struggles but they succeed. Amelia laughcries as the EMTs work on her · · · Conversations fading in and out · · · She moans. The IV is a defeat. Lego man has an iron grip on her wrists.

"Everything's gonna be fine," he insists. "The hospital is only a few blocks away."

A plain man in EMS gear tears through the supply cabinet. "We need Steristrips or liquid stitches. Her arms are a disaster."

"Why did you try to kill yourself?" asks Lego man. "Did something bad happen to you?" The horse whinnies again and the choir resumes their *oh*s and *ah*s. It takes all three of the EMTs to squeeze her wounds together and tape them shut. Lego man relaxes his grip and promises Amelia, "If you hold still we'll let you go, but not while you're fighting like this. You're making it worse."

"GOOD!" she screams, tries to tear at her wounds with her fingernails. EMTs asking her questions—her name, what day it is, who's the president—but Amelia hears only the song, the screeching and scratching of the record.

"Complete psychotic break, with extensive lacerations," the astronaut says into a radio. "Is Jason on?" A pause. "Good. Tell him to set up. He's good with this sort of thing." A little girl giggles. *The eyes are out the horse is dead.* It screams. The guitar carries her through the sliding glass doors into the Lysol-scented interior.

But the fearful, and unbelieving, and the abominable, and murderers, and whoremongers, and sorcerers, and idolaters, and all liars, shall have their part in the lake which burneth with fire and brimstone: Which is the second death.

Amelia, still wrapped in the bloody blanket, is wheeled through the doors, the horse's hooves thundering through her brain.

"Lacerations!" calls the EMT. "We called in."

A nurse scrambles out from behind a desk and says, "Yes we're set up for her in 103." They rush Amelia into a small room off the emergency ward, release her arms, and present her with a clipboard.

"Do you have insurance?" asks Lego man. She nods, dazed and overwhelmed by the extended echo of the hooves and neighs in her mind. They use the opportunity to replace the IV. "Then you need to sign this." Amelia signs it. There is blood on the paper.

"Good luck," bids the astronaut, before exiting the room with her insurance information.

NOBODY'S FAULT
(BUT MY OWN)

The music stops and her mind comes to a halt. *Hang cut stab bash
· · · Bash in the head.* She squints at the shiny instruments on a tray
under harsh lights. *I can use some of these to kill myself. Like that
syringe.* But she realizes she is not alone.

The PA is young and moves gracefully. With his sandy brown
bangs, he looks like Beck on stage. He turns on the examination
light and turns off the overhead fluorescent bulbs. *Orchestra seat-
ing.* For a moment, the examination light illuminates him like a
spotlight. She listens. *What is that instrument? An accordion? This
is a different recording. The song is tuned down a whole step from
the single. Is this the one he did in London?* The young man sits
down on a stool next to Amelia, wrapped in her bloody cocoon,
blood seeping through the Steristrips.

"My name is Jason. What's your name?"

"Amelia," she says, still guessing which version of the song she
is hearing.

"It's nice to meet you, Amelia. I'm going to take care of you.
May I see your arms?" She offers her wounds to him. Taped and
glued and bloody. *The gawky man sings in her head.*

Jason's eyes go soft with empathy. "That looks like it hurts."

"It doesn't."

He studies her, for a moment, before turning to the disinfec-
tants and stitching equipment on the tray. Amelia watches as his
delicate hands arrange the tools he will use to ruin her dreams. The

bitterness of her suicide starts to creep into her thoughts, riding on the back of Beck's words. *Blame the devil for the things you do.*

"Did you do that to yourself?" he pries. The instrument wheezes with despair.

Amelia doesn't answer. Her aural hallucination is heart-rending. Jason gently removes the blood-soaked tape from her right arm, smearing a staunching agent over the freely flowing rivulets. The ointment smells like the inside of an empty refrigerator.

Jason releases a breath, and breaks the silence. "My sister killed herself. I wish I knew why, but she didn't leave a note. She was like you—"

Amelia's eyes flash. "Was she."

"I didn't mean . . . just, she used the same . . . method."

Beck's harmonium hesitates. The musician inhales. On this incidental breath he admits that it's nobody's fault but his own. *I want to see your stomach!* Screaming · · · Her mother screamed. Her own fiancé berated her when she couldn't bear it any longer. Chris. Her gut drops. Beck continues to apologize.

Jason interrupts her song again. "Did you leave a note?"

"I mailed them all this morning."

"Them, interesting." He frowns. *Everybody's clown.* "Several notes. So how long have you been planning this?"

Amelia feels the hungry crow pecking at her nipple. "For about six months." Eight tiny claws scrabbling for purchase on her soft skin.

"So you've felt this way for a long time?"

"Since I was twelve." The nipple turns into a worm, grotesquely extended as the bird tries to choke it down.

"That's a long time to suffer," says Jason, as Amelia surreptitiously swats at her chest with her other hand, smearing blood across her collarbone. He prepares his stitching equipment. *Sew the eyelids shut. Sew the mouth shut.* He holds up a syringe. "I'll just give you this local anesthetic—"

"I don't want it." Her voice is calm, sterile.

Jason sighs, but does not argue. "Let me know if you change your mind." He places the stitches, pressing down on the fascia splitting open the hasty repair like a maggot, and pushes her skin together as he sews. It distracts her from the crow. "I'm sorry if this hurts."

"Don't worry, I'm okay," she says, monotone. *SEW THE MOUTH SHUT! Be silent, once and for all!* A clangorous piano. Make them be quiet. Make them all be quiet. They scream and wail and cry and lash out at her. Stupid fucking retard, you should have researched the nearest hospital! Should have used a sharper knife. *Shoulda got a gun.* In her mind, Jason straps her to the table and peels her skin off with a scalpel until she is as red and raw on the outside as she is on the inside.

In reality, he leans back and stretches his neck before preparing a new suture. "Now the elbow. Are you sure you don't want—"

"I'm sure. If it hurts, I deserve it." *Eloi, Eloi, lama sabachthani?*

"Ah," he sits forward. "Is that how you really feel?" Amelia nods. *SINNER.* The flesh pulls with the thread sliding through her viscera. "I don't believe that you deserve it. I don't think anyone deserves this."

It's more than I deserve.

Sew the mouth shut! Silence the apostate!

When he is done with the right arm, he moves to the other side of the table. This time he does not ask if Amelia wants anesthetic. "Somehow, in all this mess, you missed the major arteries and tendons. You're going to have some scar tissue and numbness that might hinder your dexterity, but you'll be able to write and type with minimal physical therapy. It's difficult to say because you cut some of the nerves responsible for pressure."

Amelia chokes out an excuse. "It's not as easy as they make it look in the movies, you really have to DIG in there. Things come out of you. I never thought of the skin actually holding in your tissue, but it really is the body's largest organ. . . . What a failure."

"Is this how you imagined it?" he asks.

Amelia imagines her body, pristine and cold in the afternoon sun. *Sew the mouth shut.* "No. I thought I'd be dead. I wish I had died, but the ambulance came too quickly. I miscalculated." *We can end this soon, as soon as we get back home if you'd like.* "Am I going to have to stay here after you're done?" He nods. Amelia's face crumples, but she does not cry. *KILL IT! KILL the monster · · · You fucking reeking sack of dog shit cow shit putrid rat infested—*

Beck interrupts her, reminds her again whose fault this is. *It's such a selfish way to lose.*

"There are people here who can help you."

"I don't WANT help, I want to DIE," she snaps. The crow pecks at her cornea, stabs out her left eye with its beak.

Jason speaks softly. "They're going to keep you here whether you want to stay or not. For at least three days. If you don't show improvement, longer. So it is in your best interest to get treatment and go along with the program." This morning, it seemed impossible to wait until after lunch to die. Now another three days. He ties off the last stitch. Beck's harmonium lulls her into a pain-induced meditative state. "Okay, the painful part is done. Let's wrap you up." Jason gets several pads, ointment, medical tape, and gauze. He anoints Amelia's stitches, tapes the pads over them, then wraps them up while she considers the best way to get a shotgun in Chicago. I want to be identified by my teeth.

He gestures to her inner elbows. "I'm afraid we won't be able to cover these because of the location, so get them checked once a day for inflammation."

There is a knock on the door.

"Come on in," he calls, then turns back to Amelia. "Paperwork."

PAPERWORK

A bitch in a skirt-suit, accompanied by a doctor, brusquely enters the room and flips on the fluorescent lights. Tires squealing · · · Crossing guard whistle. The music stops. She's holding a clipboard.

"You need to sign this." The bitch thrusts the clipboard at Amelia on the exam table. *The syringe is RIGHT THERE.*

"What does it say?" Amelia is immediately suspicious.

"It says you accept the mandatory treatment duration in the psychiatric ward. Three days, minimum."

The bitch has her attention.

"I'm not going to sign that," says Amelia, flatly.

The woman's lips press the corners of her mouth. "If you don't sign it, we will Baker Act you for attempted suicide."

"I didn't try to kill myself! I'm a cutter and I accidentally went too deep." A murder of crows flock to me · · · *Feast on the death.*

Images of her insides pushing up out of her skin flash behind her eyes.

The bitch throws a look across the room. "Jason?"

Jason, with his soft voice, speaks kindly to Amelia. "It will go on your permanent record if we have to put you in against your will."

"This is bullshit! I wasn't trying to kill myself!"

They stare at her in silence. GodFUCKINGdamnit! Shoulda bought a gun. *STAB in the chest* · · · *PULL out the eyes* · · · The crows are feasting · · · *TESSERACT!* Stop. Amelia regains her composure, nods at the clipboard. The bitch stabs her finger to two highlighted areas of the paper. Amelia thinks about cutting off those manicured bone spiders with pruning shears.

"Sign here and here." Amelia signs it with the taste of blood, metallic, in her mouth.

"Is that all?" *you fucking cunt-rag.*

"No," interrupts the doctor. "We need your full insurance information: provider, group number, identification number, and account holder."

"Account holder?" Amelia hesitates. "That's my father."

"Do you have your insurance card?" the doctor presses, greedy.

"I don't have anything! I don't even have clothes!" *Grab the syringe! Stab yourself in the jugular NOW!*

"Then you're going to have to call him and get the information over the phone," growls the bitch.

"No!" *Stab the jugular!* "I can't tell him! I don't have my phone, I can't tell him, I can't tell him!" Standing on Daddy's feet to dance at Aunt Nickie's wedding.

The bitch in the skirt-suit hands her a phone, breathing the stink of old smoke into Amelia's face. "Now."

::SILENCE:: There is no music to help her. No encouragement or solace. Only an unforgiving silence. Amelia takes the phone, her hands shaking, and calls her father.

"Daddy?" She pauses. "I need my insurance information, I'm at the hospital. . . . Because, because I tried to kill myself." She cries into the silence on the other end. "I'm so sorry. I'm so sorry, Daddy. Please don't tell Mom. Please don't tell anybody. . . . Yes, they're right here."

Amelia hands the phone to the bitch, who writes down everything he says in the blanks on the form. Amelia sobs. Softball practice. Canoeing in Gold Head Branch State Park. Driving eighteen hours to Chicago. Shaking hands with the president. Surrounded by the kids at the community center. There is no protection from the assault of good memories, no muting the betrayal she has committed. The only thing he ever wanted for me in life was to be happy.

And I failed even at that.

The bitch pushes the phone back into Amelia's hands. "Here."

"I'm so sorry, Daddy," she weeps. "I couldn't wait any longer—" The words stretch out of her chest like a death rattle. "I love you, too. I'm sorry."

Amelia flips the phone closed, then breaks down completely.

The doctor checks the information on the form. "Get her to processing immediately. And get her something to wear. No sleeves, no strings."

PROCESSING

"Give me the blanket," the nurse demands. The room is small and dark, except for a brightly lit white stall.

"But I don't have any clothes."

"That will just make this easier. Give me the blanket and step into the stall."

"Naked?"

"Yes, naked. I have to check for contraband." Amelia shrugs out of the bloody wrap and stands nude in the middle of the stall. The nurse stuffs the blanket into a large plastic bag and sets it to the side. "Face me." She puts on a pair of latex gloves and steps into the stall with Amelia. "Arms up." Amelia raises her arms. The nurse checks her underarms and the underside of each breast. "Arms down." Amelia complies. "Now squat."

"What?"

"Squat. Some people hide things in their private parts." Humiliated, Amelia squats. The nurse shines a flashlight between her legs. "Okay, stand back up and turn around." Tears well in Amelia's eyes. "Squat." She squats again, and the nurse, businesslike, runs a finger down the crack of Amelia's ass. A tear runs down her face. "Alright, you're safe," the nurse says, taking off the gloves. "Step on the scale, please." She writes down Amelia's weight, then measures her height. "Now give me your ring."

"My engagement ring?"

"Yes. No jewelry allowed. We'll keep it with your other belongings here in the processing room, tagged with your information, and you can have it back when you're released." Amelia pulls the ring off her finger and hands it to the nurse. She drops the ring into the bag with the blanket, then copies information from her clipboard onto the bag with a black Sharpie ::SILENCE:: There is a tanline on Amelia's ring finger. Chris. The nurse shoves the bag into a cubbyhole.

Amelia shivers. "Are you going to give me scrubs to wear or something?"

"Scrubs? No, you can hang yourself with scrubs. You get a safety gown and a pair of socks." The woman rifles through a stack of neatly folded cotton. "What size are you?"

"Four."

"Four . . . four . . ." she mumbles to herself as she goes through the clothing. "Here we are." She puts it on Amelia and gives her a once-over. "Good enough."

"Do you have any underwear?"

"You don't get underwear."

"What do you mean I don't get underwear? That's not sanitary."

"It's not safe," the nurse replies. "You hurt yourself, this is what you get: no bra, no underwear, no sleeves, no strings." Amelia wipes the tears from her face. "We're done here. I'll take you to your interview, and I'll see you again when you're discharged. Put on your socks. Let's go."

4TH OF JULY

Amelia, wearing a threadbare hospital gown fastened with Velcro, sits facing a two-way mirror. The bright white room is freezing cold, buzzing with fluorescent lights. Soundgarden's dark, distorted metal is loud in her head. I could easily throw the cold metal chair through the mirror, she thinks. Not "4th of July" anymore. No freedom eagle shotgun noose. The irony grates her nerves like Chris Cornell's voice. Stripping paint off a baseboard · · · Bubbling · · · Blistering · · · Suffocating. Amelia is staring at Mirror Amelia. Mirror Amelia is beckoning with false promises. *Smash it and use the shards to slit your throat.* They glare at each other.

The music dims when two nurses enter the room. They're wearing identical red scrub pants and have brought their own chairs. The younger nurse is shaped like a potato; the second has graying hair. Tweedledee and Tweedledum. The Jabberwock paints a grimace on the back of her teeth. What stupid-looking pants.

"So . . ." Tweedledee checks her chart. "Amelia. Why are you here?"

"Why did you try to kill yourself?" clarifies Tweedledum.

The twins' song from *Alice in Wonderland* starts playing in her head, and the nurses' movements take on a dancing quality.

"I think about killing myself every second of every day. I masturbate to thoughts of killing myself or being murdered. I'm having all kinds of impulse control problems, from spending too much money, to injuring myself, to eating more than a thousand calories a day, to angry outbursts in class. I get inconsolably upset for no reason, and often find myself standing in the hallway just weeping without knowing why. The other day I seriously considered killing myself just because of a ticking clock." The nurses stare at her. "I couldn't wait any longer."

"Wait for what?" honks Tweedledee from her bright red nose.

To shoot off half my face and set myself on fire to get the plastic skin · · · The folded magazine-gloss Saran Wrap. It always sticks to itself. To bake my feet into shoes and my breasts into armor.

"Death."

Tweedledee gets out a pen. "Please answer these questions truthfully. Have you intentionally hurt yourself before?"

This is the least comfortable chair I've ever sat in. Let it be known that this day, in room 204 at St. Thomas Hospital in Chicago, Illinois, I, Amelia Adams, experienced the world's least comfortable chair.

"Yes. I used to burn myself to prove to God that I was worthy of redemption."

A chair of broken glass and sticks would be better.

"Turns out I wasn't."

The cartoon on the left scribbles. "Ever used any drugs?"

"Alcohol and marijuana; that's it."

On fire, even.

"Do you have a history of physical abuse?"

"No."

"Sexual abuse?"

"Never."

"Did you have a plan for your suicide, or was it a spur-of-the-moment decision?"

"I've dreamed about it for ten years. I've planned it for about six months."

Tweedledee scribbles. Amelia listens to the song.

"Have you ever been told you have a mental condition?"

"Does being told I'm possessed count?"

Bloody cross. GUILTY! You fucking sadist · · · *You fucking death cult god-head—*

"How have you been sleeping?" asks Tweedledum.

"I get up at five a.m., work six to nine, class ten to four, then homework six to ten. But I'm not tired; I just naturally don't need a lot of sleep."

"Any disordered eating?"

"I thought I could starve myself to death, but it was taking too long." Tweedledee frowns and makes notes. Cretius starved himself to death. A Gregorian chant begins, dissonant against the background of Soundgarden. The vocal chords · · · *See the vocal chords. Enter* · · · *Get inside, see the inside.* Would the heart be warm? *slipstinkslickshit* Would her eyes roll into whites and reds, soft and terrified behind CoverGirl lashes?

Tweedledum pipes up, "Did you only restrict or did you binge and purge as well?"

"Restriction only. I think bulimics are hypocrites."

The nurse circles something on her paper. "What about invasive thoughts or racing thoughts?"

"Yes."

"When? What about?"

"Right now. All the time. Mostly music. And cutting my eyes out of my face; the sound of popping them in my hands makes me cringe, but I obsess over it." She mimes the motion with her hands. *Take out the eyes!* "Cutting up the face. Something shattering into my face and doing the equivalent." *Exploding windshield.* "It's compulsive, now. I see an iron and I think about burning myself. I see a lamp cord and I think about hanging. Every object I encounter, I scan for its potential to harm me. Also, I hear and see things sometimes that are not really there. And sometimes think things that are not true."

"Do you ever hear voices?" asks Tweedledum.

"I can't really describe them as 'voices.' They're more like very specific, unique perspectives that appear as loud thoughts, but they all seem to be Me, as a Gestalt. So I have all these perspectives; some agree with some, some disagree with everyone, and some are cowards who can never make a decision. They hate my favoritism, so a lot of decisions I put into the hands of chance. Like the other day I was walking to a pottery museum and one part said, 'You're tired, you should take the shortcut,' but then another was like, 'Shortcut? You're a fucking fatass. There's no way we're taking a shortcut,' so my main perspective decided to walk in the opposite direction of the old lady in front of us, and that settled the matter." *You're still a fatass.* "It is NOT as if I am thinking over the problem or considering other options. It's as if I'm in a room full of people arguing."

Amelia pauses.

"I can almost always tell the difference between the voices in my head and the real world. But some are malicious. Sometimes I hear whispers and curses when walking down the aisle at the grocery store, and figures hulk in the corners of my mind, telling me to tear out the eyes." *DESTROY THE EYES!* "Plus things like hearing the doorbell ring, even though we don't have a doorbell. Telephones. Seeing bats flying at my face, mailboxes that move, reflections that don't. There's this crow that follows me around. I can't taste my food, and I spent three months convinced I was pregnant with a dead fetus. Everything looks two-dimensional, and the constant music can be very distracting."

"You've mentioned music twice. What music?" honks Tweedledee.

"You know, the music you can hear in your head. Sometimes mine gets too loud and everything else gets drowned out. The worst part is the earworms."

He's got the whole wo-rld / in His hands /

"Fuck! I've just gotten one stuck in my head just by thinking about it!" Amelia puts her fingers in her ears and hums the *I Dream of Jeannie* theme song.

Duh DAH / in His hands / Duh DAH in / duh dat-dat duh / Duh DAH, DAT da dat-dat da DA! / bum-bum bum bum / Bum, bum-bum

She opens her eyes with a look of relief.

The Tweedletwins are bewildered.

"Any major life changes recently?" asks Tweedledee, turning to the second page.

"No. Well, I'm getting married soon, but we've been together since ninth grade, so that's not really 'recent.'" Chris. Eight years of memories flood her brain. *Sew the mouth shut.*

"Any absenteeism from work or school?"

"Yeah. I failed out of most of my classes this semester because I couldn't sit still long enough. Lost my scholarship."

Tweedledee makes a mark on the paper. "Any reckless behavior?"

"I guess."

"Like what?"

"Like . . ." The images flicker into Amelia's mind in a rush. "Speeding down the highway at night with my headlights off, driving behind trucks with poorly secured ladders for miles just in case one falls off and crashes through my windshield, walking around bad neighborhoods at one in the morning when I can't sleep, plugging in appliances soaking wet." She smiles, humorless. "Flying AirTran."

Tweedledee scribbles. Amelia imagines using the pen to stab herself in the neck.

"When was the last time you felt happy?"

"I guess about a decade ago? I had a wonderful childhood, but when puberty hit, everything changed." *Repent! Repent! Beg God's forgiveness for your nasty thoughts and wickedness!* "Everything in here," she taps her temple.

"Are there times you feel like you have more energy? Are more creative? Have a higher sex drive?"

"Yes, but I don't feel happy; I feel dangerous and out of control." Tango on the dance floor. Guns · · · So many guns · · · *Shoulda used a gun.*

Tweedledee keeps up the line of questioning. "And how long do those feelings usually last?"

"Weeks. Months."

Tweedledum nods and writes. "Are there periods of neutrality between these episodes?"

"If feeling like a robot counts as neutral, then yes. If you mean not wanting to die, then no."

Eeeevvvvvvveee . . . hisses the serpent.

"Tell me about your hygiene."

"Sometimes I shower once a week and go for days without brushing my teeth. Sometimes I shower three times a day and brush my gums til they bleed. It all depends on my mood."

"And your sex drive?"

"That varies, too. But I still have sex with my fiancé even when I don't want to, because it's not fair for me to take my feelings out on him."

"Last question, then we'll get you a room. How are you spending your leisure time?"

Amelia stares at her bandages. "Reading, running, skateboarding, playing with my dog, playing the piano, writing, listening to music, sitting on the floor of the shower until the water gets cold, watching faces move in the marble. . . . Anything to take my mind off it."

"Interesting." They take turns signing the bottom of the clipboard. "Thank you for talking with us, Amelia. Please excuse us for a minute."

The twins bounce out of the room on big rubber bottoms.

"In His Hands" plays in Amelia's head again. She considers the importance of the Jack-in-the-box when vomiting. Caulrophobia. Everybody's clown.

He's got the whole wo-rld /

The loneliness that comes when you're in a room full of people

in His hands /

and you are so mentally devastated that you can't entertain anyone

He's got the whole wo-rld /

or even find the volition to ask for a glass of water

in His hands /

so certain you are that you will get a glass of milk instead.

He's got the whole wo-rld /

Everyone else has the gift of speech but they only stare at you in your incapacity

in His hands /

and wait for the punchline.

He's got the whole world in His hands

Do something interesting, Amelia!

Say something interesting, Amelia!

Everybody's clown.

Only Tweedledum returns. "We'll get you set up in the secure ward. There's a group movement session going on right now, then dinner, two hours of free time, then lights out. You'll see the doctor in three days."

"Three days? That's when I'm supposed to be discharged!"

The nurse pauses with her hand on the door. "You're a high-risk case and you will stay here for at least two weeks." She opens the door so Amelia can step into the hallway with her, then locks it behind them.

FRIENDLY CHARLIE

Tweedledum ushers Amelia down a dingy hallway, the stench of human urine on the side of Harold's Chicken Shack on Wabash Avenue. She wrinkles her sensitive nose.

"It smells like piss."

"Well, it's not the fanciest place in Chicago, but I think you'll get what you need here." Amelia's stomach turns.

He's got the little bitty babies / in His hands /
He's got the little bitty babies / in His hands /
He's got the little bitty babies / in His hands /
He's got the whole world in His hands

They reach a large common room filled with an odd assortment of people. Amelia is the only one in a "safety gown." *You belong here you sick piece of shit.* A few people are in various stages of stretching within a rectangle formed by two dilapidated couches and a spindly wooden chair. *Go make friends with the Isle of Misfit Toys. TAKE OUT THE EYES!* There are lightweight plastic card tables along the walls, accompanied by lightweight plastic chairs. Two people occupy each corner of a Goodwill-reject sofa. The crow's claws dig into her shoulder. It bobs its head. Amelia cringes at the New Age music playing on a small CD player next to the therapist. It sounds tinny to her auditory palate. Wimpy, limp massage hands · · · What the fuck did you think? Rachael and the olives.

Tweedledum tells Amelia, "This is the therapeutic movement session. Every Tuesday and Thursday from five to six."

Amelia is silent. I might be able to crack a sharp shard from the chair. *Stab out the eyes.* Nothing really to do with the plastic tables and chairs. Maybe I can break the glass if there's a TV.

"It's fun! At least, it's better than sitting around being bored."

Could there be wires in the sofa?

As soon as Tweedledum leaves, Amelia is accosted by a thin, graying, older man. He jumps off the couch, menacing and grandiose, speaking rapidly · · · *Obscenely graphic life-size wooden crucifix* · · · There is no escape from this man's tenacious, lined face, his wild eyes.

"Hey what's your name? I'm Maxwell, what're you in for, what're you in for? I'm in here for—" And here his voice goes sotto voce. "—drugs. What're you in . . ." He suddenly yanks Amelia's right arm and examines the stitches on her inner elbow. He squeezes, hard, a mean glint in his eyes. *HURT the bitch! STAB the bitch · · · Rip out her stitches RIP HER STITCHES OUT!* She thinks she sees a third, reptilian eyelid flash across his eyes. "We have a cutter!" he yells, gleefully. "We have a cutter, ladies and gentlemen, an attention-seeking freak! Give her attention! Give her attention!"

The movement therapist in downward-facing dog lifts her head up to look at the man. "Sit down, please, Max."

Amelia wishes he would strangle her to death, but he only grins through tar-stained teeth. "You can have my seat, freak. Charlie won't mind." Maxwell points to the open space on a decrepit couch, next to a young man with a likable face. Amelia sits. Goddamnit I am sick of blue eyes.

Chris.

::PANIC::

I'll be dead, soon. I'll be really dead soon and I won't even have to talk to him.

The movement session continues and Amelia searches her mind for a song to drown it out. Why don't they just play classical music? She tunes in to the third movement of "Moonlight Sonata." Fast. Vigorous. Only Amelia and the handsome young man are not participating.

"I like your hair," he says under his breath.

Amelia looks at him sideways. "Thanks. It was an accident." She considers telling him the story of how her dyed black hair wouldn't relinquish the color, and how she slowly created the white roots, red shafts, and black ends that hang down to her waist, but she cannot manage even an intentional breath, so she stays silent and listens to Beethoven.

When the unclean spirit has gone out of a person, it wanders through waterless regions looking for a resting place, but it finds none. Then it says, 'I will return to my house from which I came.' When it comes, it finds it empty, swept, and put in order. Then it goes and brings along seven other spirits more evil than itself, and they enter and live there; and the last state of that person is worse than the first.

Amelia and Charlie sit quietly while the movement therapist encourages the others to stand in tree pose. The disembodied hands type a message on an ancient typewriter, roll up the paper, cork it in a bottle, and send it out to sea.

"Charlie, why don't you help our new friend become a tall, relaxed tree?"

Amelia lashes out with her forked tongue, "I don't want to be a tree. I want to die."

"Well . . . just don't want you two to miss out!" says the woman balancing on one leg.

Charlie finds the bottle on a distant shore and opens it. It says
MURDER ME? CIRCLE ONE: YES OR NO.

Amelia sits and stares at the wall. Look at all these fucking Dasein. Maybe if I had taken home economics in middle school . . . or ballet. I don't know what could have been done different that could have saved me from this lovelessness and self-hate. Nothing. I am here in this absurd, self-righteous world with all the other Dasein. Bored out of my mind just like all the other Dasein. Silent like a snot-nosed cow staring bleary-eyed into a water-sheet mirage of hot desert air. *DIE DIE DIE DIE!* At least I got a bikini wax. The slut's equivalent of wearing a clean pair of underwear.

Two large, metal carts pushed by orderlies squeal down the hallway. Amelia's body contracts at the sound of the three bad wheels · · · Knives in her tympanic membrane. Beethoven gets louder in an attempt to drown out the screeching wheels.

Charlie smiles. "Now you get to see the REAL freak show: dinner time."

THE FREAK SHOW

The carts smell like blood. Taste it · · · Metallic. Maxwell is wildly gesticulating while talking to the orderlies. He convinces them to let him hand out the trays of food. "For the retard!" Maxwell slides a tray in front of a Hispanic woman. "For the nun!" That one is for a woman already in the stages of prayer. *Cut out the eyes.* He is balancing several trays of food, and sliding each one to the person described. "For the schizo! For the darkie! For the zombie!"

Then a demon-oppressed man who was blind and mute was brought to him, and he healed him, so that the man spoke and saw.

The grisly wind-burnt figure whirls toward Charlie and Amelia at their own table. "For the lady . . ." he says with a curtsy, setting a tray in front of Charlie. "And last, and certainly least, the attention-seeking freak." Her food bounces sickeningly when the tray makes contact with the table. *Jack-in-the-box.*

Amelia raises her eyebrows to Charlie. "Lady?"

"I'm in here for bulimia," admits the young man. *Jack-in-the-box.* Maxwell scampers away. *Split the cow. Crack her empty-open rib cage yawning · · · Roaring swallowing insects and long white arms. Up to the elbows. We're up to the elbows in blood.* Amelia sniffs her food. *Fat fucking piece of shit pig ass disgusting piece of shit. It doesn't need to eat.*

She agrees with herself. "Looks like cafeteria food." The insides are on the outside now. *Look at the fat, the puke, the waste.*

"It's not too bad on the way up," he shrugs.

Hypocrite, she thinks.

"You can have mine."

"No, I can't. They record everything you eat for each meal; sharing is 'strictly prohibited.'" The rest of the sonata seems droll at the moment. Beethoven trails off into tuneless humming.

For several minutes, they sit across from each other, poking their food with sporks. Unable to conjure another song, she entertains herself with prime numbers. 1, 2, 3, 5, 7, 11, 13, 17, 19, 23 · · · Now, 23 · · · That's a great number because 2+3=5 which is also a prime number. Lucky number for softball, but not soccer. 173 is similar, only it's 11, of course. 181, 191, 193, 197, 199, 211 . . . Her mind skims through numbers like index cards and lands on 457, her absolute favorite number of all time. It's my favorite time of day, she tells Charlie in her head. Dusk. Gravestones. I wanted to kill myself on 4/5/2007 at 4:57 but 1) I couldn't wait that long and 2) That would be my brother's birthday.

In a sudden fit of fear, a young Latino guy picks up his tray and starts smashing at imaginary somethings all around him. Demons? Like mine? *No. Your suffering is unspectacular.* Amelia watches as three tall male orderlies approach the teen, talking to him in low, calm voices.

Right then, Maxwell points to an innocuous spot on the wall and shouts, "Pedro, LOOK OUT!" The young man collapses in terror with a scream. The orderlies descend upon him. Amelia's mind-crows caw and beat their wings. *DIE! DIE! DIE!* they scream.

She turns to Charlie. "How can I be the freak with all these psychos in here? I thought suicide was a pretty common thing in the psych ward."

"Nah," he says, tearing apart a roll. "You've got mostly your schizos, bipolars, and homeless people. Rosemary is a syphilitic. I don't know what the fuck is up with her." He gestures to Lucia, still performing an elaborate blessing over her meal. "But she never shuts the fuck up. Juanita there is a mute. John Doe lives here, if you call what he does 'living.' Maxwell's just a maniac. I don't know the black guy."

There will be something in the room. There will be something in the room you can use to hang yourself, or electrocute yourself, and this will all be over soon. *Carve out a new throat. A new smile, red and luscious and writhing with worms.*

A squat, middle-aged nurse with dark hair and a sharp face approaches with a clipboard. She does not introduce herself. Amelia dislikes her immediately. Shave off that hair. Piles of brunette.

The woman stops in front of their table and scowls at Amelia. "You're not eating."

"I'm not hungry," she says, the acrid smoke of burnt hair in the back of her nostrils.

"No?" The nurse flips through the charts. "That's funny because your chart says that you're trying to starve yourself to death, but you just said you're 'not hungry.' What am I supposed to believe?" Amelia stares into the nurse's eyes and imagines slicing the fat off her stomach in thick chunks. Her head-fingers feel sticky. "Well, since you're not eating anyway . . ." She snatches up Amelia's tray and walks away.

By . . . MEN-nen

Charlie leans forward. "She's always a bitch, and she'll steal your stuff, so be careful."

"I don't have any stuff."

"I'm just saying she obviously hates her job and wants everyone else to be miserable, too—"

All I need is an electrical cord and a surface to anchor it.

"—the rest of the staff is okay."

The kindergarteners have a lot to say about Maxwell, but the disembodied hands are more interested in Charlie. *All of you shut the fuck up,* she orders them. They respond with ugly faces and rude gestures. Lucia places her tray into its designated slot in the rolling cart. *We all need to focus. We're not living one second longer than we must.*

The old woman named Rosemary summons an orderly as if he were a servant. He scurries like a little white mouse in his uniform. Hotel bellhops. Dancing sailors in *Anything Goes.* Most of the patients take out decks of playing cards and have their trays collected from them. Maxwell throws his across the room, mocking the staff as they clean up.

Charlie slides his tray to the edge of the table. "So, do you want a smoke? We're allowed in the smoking lounge five times a day—when we get up, after breakfast, lunch, dinner, and then right before lights out." Black lungs sticky with tar. Chemotherapy. She imagines her bald head. Now can you love me? asks a proud Lenox figurine.

"Smoking is a long, ugly, disgusting death. I could get cancer just sitting in there."

Charlie laughs. "You're in here because you want to die, but you're worried about cigarettes?"

"Like I said, it's a long, slow, ugly death. No thanks."

"Suit yourself." He shrugs, stands up, and walks to the lounge.

THE VALLEY

A handsome orderly approaches Amelia, who vaguely considers sucking his dick on first sight. "Amelia?" he asks. She nods and gags a little in her fantasy. "I'm Daniel. Come on, I'll show you to your room." Amelia gets up, shakes his hand, and follows Daniel down the hall.

Peel me away from you. I am your skin, clinging. I am naked at your feet. I am sucking your cock. I am spent in your arms and you never give me what I want. I am touching you. I want to kill myself, and I would have to rip them out. RIP OUT THE EYES. I HATE them. Rip out the gray-pink mass inside and tear my brain out through my nose like the Egyptians did. Tear off my face. Cut off my feet so that I balance on hysterical rectangular stumps. Tear out new tear ducts · · · *Burrow into my face and end it all. I could stab myself in the face eight times.*

Then would you love me?

Of course not. She lowers her eyes to Daniel's shoes. *But, you know . . . the option is there.* He makes me want to cut off my breasts. Lop them off. *Because you don't deserve them.* Yes. *Because he probably hates them.* Yes, yes, I feel it ::SHIVER:: *I hate you.* The feeling is mutual.

"You're in 4D. Your roommate's name is Hailey. She's about your age but has difficulty communicating. She'll be discharged tomorrow." Thick and veined · · · *Sew the mouth shut.* Demons screaming in orgasm · · · *That's how I feel every time you sin against Me.* They arrive at the room marked 4D. "Here you are. Good luck," he says, and walks back toward the common room.

Her curiosity piques in octaves **G#—G# 8ᵛᵃ** Amelia looks for a knob, but sees only a keyhole **G#—G#8ᵛᵃ** Ravel **G#—G# 8ᵛᵃ** "La vallée des cloches." She pushes through the song to open the door, which is on a recessed hinge, and notices that the corners are rounded downward.

She steps in and immediately searches the room for suicide options.

They won't have curtains but there should be knobs. There are no knobs. There should be . . .

Her eyes do a preliminary check.

Nothing. The piano booms halfway through measure eight · · · Sinister and dissonant **B natural** Her eyes bounce from empty space to empty space. **E#** hits her three times in the chest. All of her expected suicide options are missing. No lamps or fans. No electrical cords **E# E# E#** The dressers are recessed shelves **E# E# E#** There are no bars on the window like in the movies. The metal is crisscrossed within the glass, which appears thick and shatterproof. There are no curtains or blinds, not a single cord.

Amelia moves with the song in 5/4 to the adjacent bathroom. Pianissimo. The bathroom is large and clean, but the faucet for the sink is rounded forward, and there is no plug. Down a half-step. The toilet flush is a button against the wall that you press. There has to be SOMETHING · · · I am not living like this one minute longer. The shower has no curtain, liner, or door. The water is operated by a push button with no temperature adjustments. The toilet is accompanied by a plastic chair tucked into the corner. What about the bed?

Ravel modulates into a major key, and Amelia searches the sleeping area, desperate. There has to be something! The full bed is flush against the wall and only a few inches off the floor **B♭ B♭ B♭** No headboard and the wood beneath is smooth and rounded **B♭ B♭ B♭** A single, flat pillow; no pillowcase; a waterproof fitted sheet attached to the mattress **B♭ B♭ B♭** There is nothing to use as a noose. There is nothing she can attach it to. They've thought of everything.

No corners.

No bars.

No faucets.

No hinges.

No cords.

No sheets.

No sleeves.

No strings.

Her heartbeat skips along with the syncopation.

She is going to have to live.

An orderly knocks on the door, robbing her of Ravel's empathy.

"Someone is on the phone for you, Amelia, named Chris. You have ten minutes to complete your conversation."

DON'T LEAVE ME NOW

Pink Floyd's "Don't Leave Me Now" floats into her skull along with Chris's name. Two measures of each bizarre chord progression plods through her head. A song without a key. She stands up, numb, gliding toward the orderly in the doorway. The roots form a pair of tritones. The Devil's chord. *Slash and lick slash and lick. Greedy! Selfish! Whore fuckslutcumdumpster piece of shit trash . . .*

Sinner . . . hisses the serpent.

Amelia finds her way to the pay phone attached to the wall in the corridor, closely watched by the orderly. *Stab out the eyes. Sew the eyes shut. Sew the eyes OPEN. Watch it. Watch the devil slice you to ribbons and fuck the bloody meat sack that's left.* There is a long pause. Her voice slips between the cracks in the song.

"Hello?"

A cold silence, then, "Hey."

The song fills in the spaces.

"I don't know what to say. I'm so sorry—"

A flood of sound a thousand miles away comes pouring from his mouth. "You wait until I'm out of town visiting my father who has cancer and you slash your fucking wrists? Something in you thought that would be a good idea, that that would somehow make things easier for me?"

"You know I've felt this way for a long time," she begins as the lyrics beg for forgiveness. "I can't help it. I told you a thousand times, the music and voices, they won't stop. I couldn't take it anymore."

"You couldn't take what?" He is furious. "Having great friends and a great life and a great family? And you wait until now? You're so fucking selfish it's ASTOUNDING. This is the last thing I need right now, to deal with your mental problems while my father is dying."

"I'm sorry!" Roger Waters's voice cracks under her words. "I'm sorry. I thought I wouldn't have to explain this. I sent a letter."

"Yeah? And what did it say? Did it say 'I could have done this at ANY other time, ANY other time and I would have been at your side'? 'Sorry I didn't wait for you to bury your father because I can't control myself'? 'Sorry I grew up with everything I ever wanted and still managed to come out defective'?"

"No, it said I love you and I'm sorry if it causes you any pain to lose me, but I hoped you'd understand that I would finally have peace and silence." A poor retelling. She spent weeks crafting those letters, writing in her best calligraphy.

He scoffs. "Peace and silence. That's funny because my dad is on a morphine drip and he has plenty of peace and silence."

"I wish I DID have cancer so that I could finally die!"

Instant regret.

His anger swells, screaming with the song. "You are so goddamn melodramatic. You have such unearned pain. I don't get it. If you did it because you need attention, I could understand, but you have this sick hatred of it that is so much worse. You're spoiled and ungrateful and weak."

"I'm not weak! I've survived this shit for ten years! I ENDURED. But then I stayed up til four a.m. picking imaginary maggots out of our carpet—slimy rice-size maggots squirming through the carpets in the bedroom—and I drowned them in a plate of pancake syrup. And you know what? In the morning nothing was in the syrup."

Shock. Vomit. *Don't trust the government.*

"That does not, in any way, excuse what you have done."

"Chris, please!"

"Listen to me you psycho bitch, this is the worst thing you could've ever done to me. I will never forgive you for this. I hope I never see your face again."

"Are you . . . are you leaving me? We're supposed to get married in September."

Burning alive in a wedding dress.

"How can you possibly expect me to marry you after this? You think I'm just going to pretend this never happened? I'll never be able to trust you again."

Drums, bass, and guitar all enter. They hit Amelia like a shockwave.

She rushes her words together, fanning the flames. "Please don't do this. I told you, I tried to tell you that night, that last night together before you left, and I cried and you asked what was wrong. You ASKED and I told you I felt like killing myself and you said—"

"I said what? I said you should see a counselor, like I have a million times before, and—"

"We can't afford it!" she sobs.

"If I hadn't bought you that car for your birthday we'd be able to afford it."

The crow picks at her charred flesh.

"It doesn't help! I don't have anything to talk about. It's like you said, my life is perfect—"

He interrupts her with the skill of a practiced manipulator. "Your life IS perfect, so you are either the most selfish bitch on the planet, or something happened in your childhood that you need to fucking deal with, which means you would be LYING to me.

45

Which is it? Are you lying about wanting to die, or lying about your past?"

"You know I've told you everything, I had no other choice! There's no escape, I can't stand it anymore, I had to make a decision!" Her head is swarming with confusion and noise.

"Yeah, you made a decision. So here's my decision: I'm not going to forgive you. I'm not going to marry you. In fact, I hope you DO kill yourself and go straight to Hell where you belong. Goodbye."

Dial tone.

Amelia tunes in to the song in her head. The phone drops from her hand and dangles on its cord.

Click.

Voices.

Click.

Hang yourself with the phone cord.

Clickclick

It's too short.

Clickclickclickclick—

The sounds of the universe cannot block it out.

Get it out, get it out of my head!

Amelia screams inside.

RADIO-HEAD

Amelia lies on her bed, with her meager pillow and too-short blanket. She is switching music in her head, trying to find the right radio station. John Lee Hooker, she orders her brain, and several songs fade in and out, but none stick. She tries Led Zeppelin, Massive Attack, Bach, Danny Elfman. Nothing but static.

There is a loud *click* and the radio turns off.

The crow scratches at her eyeballs with its claws.

Silence invades Amelia's head like mustard gas.

She closes her eyes and it's there: a rabbit wrapped in electrical tape and dripping with tar. Backlit by an open doorway, it stares at her without eyes, six huge, curved talons flick out from its right hand. Its left hand is a powerful black paw with short, strong fingers · · · Only five · · · Like a hand without an opposable thumb.

She opens her eyes to escape the vision.

The clock is ticking.

Why can't I think of a fucking **All around the mulberry bush /** No fuck you, NO, a SONG.

She closes her eyes.

Another creature is in the monster's room. The tar rabbit stares at the knotted child-shaped tree, ever silent ::FLICKFLICKFLICK:: *Tick. Tick. Tick.* The tree-child's arms are crossed over its chest, molded into the bark like the woven branches of a ficus. *Tick. Tick. Tick.* Without warning, the rabbit attacks, rakes its claws along the tree-child's scalp then viciously slashes at its shoulders from behind. The bark heals when the talons retract, leaving behind a light-green cicatrix. It is growing imperceptibly.

There is no rabbit.

::FLICK::

Tick.

Full-out war.

The monster attacks, the tree heals. The rabbit opens its huge maw and gouges the serenely closed eyes of the tree-child, ripping out chunks with its fangs, the shredded eye sockets heal into knots. And now they are both blind. The rabbit's plastic-constricted chest heaves with satisfaction. *Tick* ::FLICK:: *Tick* ::FLICK:: *Tick* ::FLICK:: In another flash, it stabs its six long claws straight into the tree-child's face and yanks upwards, splitting the head into seven splinters ::FLICKFLICKFLICK::

Amelia opens her eyes.

Tick. Tick. Tick.

Tick.

Tick.

Tick.

Pink Floyd conjures more clocks, intensifying the urgency. With each second, the ticking seems louder and louder until it is intolerable. Eyes closed, the back of her eyelids burst with geometric patterns when "Time" erupts in her eardrums.

The dissonant clangor of ringing in her head propels her out of bed. She runs through the door to the side of the nurses' station, reaches up, and pulls the clock off the wall. It makes an audible ripping sound · · · Attached by Velcro. Shit! Someone's coming. As quickly as possible, Amelia removes the batteries from the clock and throws them in the trash ::SILENCE:: The tiny muscles between her ribs and breastbone relax, and she breathes easily. Then, an ancient voice yells from several doors down.

"I need to wash my vagina!" It echoes down the hallway. What the fuck was that? "My vagina is so dirty! It's so dirty it needs to be washed NOW! NOW! NOW NOW NOW!"

A plump, black orderly scurries toward Amelia, who rushes to put the clock back into place. They're going to chart me for leaving my room, she thinks, but the orderly only passes her with a warning.

"Back into bed, please. This is only gonna escalate."

The senescent voice screeches again. "I'm going in the shower right now, whether you're here or not! I might slip and fall and break my hip, and then I'm gonna sue the shit out of this place!" Amelia slips back into her room, but the old woman's voice is barely muffled by the door. "Not you, you fucking nigger!" *Ooooooo* . . . chorus the kindergarteners.

The black female orderly speaks from five doors away. "Rosemary, I'm here to help—"

"You just want to see my vagina! You're a dyke," she jeers. "You want to see it because all you've seen is nigger pussy!"

Curling into a fetal position on her bed, Amelia does her best to block out the conversation.

"It's time to go to sleep. You should have showered before lights out."

"I heard it's purple," Rosemary goads her. "Is nigger pussy really purple?"

Amelia pulls her short blanket up over her ears, which exposes her feet.

"Please don't say that word. It's not the kind of thing you say to people."

"What? Nigger or pussy? Nigger nigger nigger nigger pussy pussy pussy!"

Amelia's brain has been shocked into silence. "You WANT to see my vagina! You WANT to wash it!"

A voice calls out. "Ain't nobody want to see your wrinkly ass nasty ass vagina!" and suddenly the whole ward is awake. Lucia begins wailing prayers in Spanish. Amelia hears Maxwell yelling from the men's hall on the other side of the nurses' station, demanding to know whether or not black women have purple vaginas.

Amelia puts her pillow and blanket around her ears and turns her internal radio back on, finally finding peace in Marilyn Manson.

A BEAUTIFUL MORNING

Amelia snaps awake. For a few moments, she ponders the motes of dust in a shaft of morning sun; violins sweet in her head. But then the orchestra enters. Oh my God no. The song begins. No no no · · · None of that. It continues, unabated. Amelia tries to squeeze her brain shut, but Rodgers and Hammerstein pick at her cerebral scabs.

Oooooooooooh

Amelia grimaces. No.

Oooooooooooh

Please no.

Oooooooooooh

She takes a deep breath.

"Oh, What a Beautiful Mornin'" has been unleashed upon her.

She rushes out of the room in her thin hospital gown. Charlie is already at a table meant for two-player card games. She sits with him, exhausted, Gordon McRae happily riding a horse through her head.

He gives her a grim smile. "Quite a show last night, huh? My favorite part was when someone told that old bitch no one wanted to see her wrinkly ass vagina. Fucking classic."

"Is that kind of thing normal in this place?"

The second verse starts.

Charlie nods. "Oh yeah. I've probably slept a total of twelve hours since I've been here."

"Great. That's just fucking great."

"That's just fucking hyperbole, Amelia. You'll get used to it."

Ooooooooooh · · · Amelia furrows her brow and covers her eyes. What the actual fuck? Are you really gonna sing this whole fucking song? The orderlies roll in the food carts. Amelia's ears hone in on exactly which wheels are making the screeching noise this time, stopping the song.

Maxwell swoops in to help distribute trays. "What've we got here? Eggs Benedict? Belgian waffles? Bagels and lox? Nooo . . . just scrambled powdered eggs, toast, hash, and coffee. My favorite." He casts a nasty look at Amelia, his third eyelid sliding back across his eyes. "Are you gonna let the freak have a knife to spread butter on her toast?" Amelia lies with her face, as if she isn't hoping for serrated plastic to saw open her flesh. The orderly rolls his bored, brown eyes.

"Everyone's toast has already been buttered, Max." The food trays are handed out, and she scans her plate. The toast is dried human skin. Eggs are bird fetuses, hash browns are fingernail clippings · · · *and rat feces* · · · and rat feces. Charlie gauges Amelia's expression and agrees with her silent disappointment.

"I don't understand why they give us this shit. My parents are paying four hundred dollars a day for me to be in here, and this only makes me want to eat less." Her stomach turns at the smell of preservatives.

"Charlie, you seriously have the perfect body."

"That's because I throw up after I eat." *Jack-in-the-box.*

He motions for her to pick up the toast, but she says, "Just coffee for me. What is Maxwell doing?"

Maxwell is going from patient to patient, whispering in their ears, then gulping down their coffee. Amelia watches in horror as he steals the mute woman's coffee and downs it. Charlie shrugs.

"Oh that's his usual morning routine: drinking all the coffee he can get his hands on."

"Yes! Yes! I think that's a record, folks. SIIIIXXX!" yells Maxwell triumphantly. "Sexy sixy, sexy sixy!" he chants, gyrating his hips.

Amelia drags her eyes back to the Styrofoam plate.

"So . . . they let him, of all people, consume everyone's coffee first thing in the morning?"

"Every single day," he replies, chewing a piece of toast. "Anything he does before noon is entirely their fault." An awkward silence shoves the song back into Amelia's ears. There is an uncomfortable silence for him, but for Amelia there is only the song. "Well . . . tell me about yourself," he says.

It pauses again.

"Hm. Well, if I had to choose between being deaf or blind, I would choose blind . . . even though you're supposed to say deaf due to things like balance and adaptation. If there's one thing I wish I could live without, it's eating. I would give up ten years of my life to be permanently twenty pounds thinner. I can play six instruments and sing in eight different languages. If I were guaranteed not to get caught, I would kill a person for ten million dollars."

She blinks and sees the girl: head bashed in, teeth through the cheek, unrecognizable as a face · · · Body bruised and broken, heaving lungs torn by the sharp shards of shattered ribs. In an instant all that, and then opens her eyes to escape to the light. She blinks again and the skull is shining pink and white between mats of hair. Her gums are black already, and one eye, terrified and begging · · · Flailing . . .

"I think rapists and child molesters should be castrated. I would like to develop excellent night vision. I am bisexual. In life, I am still most impressed by love. My greatest fear is being tortured by dentists dressed up as clowns." *Rip out the liar's teeth.* "My favorite cereal is Cinnamon Toast Crunch, and my favorite color is black, then red. I'm afraid to have children because I don't want them to suffer like I suffer, and every day for ten years I wake up in the morning wishing I hadn't." Charlie swallows the eggs in his mouth before she asks, "You?"

"Um, like I said, I'm here for bulimia. It's not uncommon among wrestlers. I guess it started in middle school—"

Amelia interrupts him. "I don't want to know about your disorder. I want to know about you."

He pauses to collect his thoughts, then starts again, "Okay, um, I'm nineteen. I'm an only child. I got an athletic scholarship to Northwestern and moved here from Indiana. I'm from Indiana . . ." He's not sure what else to say, and the conversation lapses back into silence for him, and *Oklahoma!* for her.

Nurse Rhonda appears, scowling at Amelia's tray. "No food this morning. Interesting. This will be noted."

Amelia turns on her. "Why don't you note Maxwell drinking six cups of coffee instead of worrying about whether or not I subject myself to this shit you people call 'food'?" *you fucking cow.*

Nurse Rhonda turns on Charlie. "Charlie, are you encouraging this behavior?"

"No!" he says, innocent hands in the air. *Choke the boy.*

"Better not be. You want to get out of here, don't you?" She gives Charlie a saccharine smile as Amelia imagines what she would look like with a full beard and bat wings.

"Of course. I'll try to be a better influence." *Strangle the boy.*

"Good," judges the nurse. "Smoking lounge is open. Free time til ten o'clock."

THE REMOTE (PART I)

Everyone is gathered around the television as a creepy choir of children recite the rosary, led by an Irish nun. Amelia isn't watching, but she can hear every word from the opposite end of the room. Each repetition sears a new scar on her heart · · · The love poems to that god · · · That brutal dictator who has abused Amelia half her life. Is this some sort of sick, cosmic joke? She hails a nurse.

"Can you please turn this shit off? It's been stuck on the Catholic channel for seventy-two hours. If I have to hear the Lord's Prayer one more time, I'm gonna put my head through that television."

A voice comes from behind a newspaper, "Someone already tried that." A middle-aged black man with glasses sits on a couch facing away from the television. Amelia squints at the TV and sees that it is bolted to the wall under a shield of Plexiglass. The nurse turns up her nose.

"I'm sorry, but I'm not in charge of things like the remote."

"The remote?" An orderly pops up.

A man at the counter answers him. "Yeah, you seen it?"

"No," the orderly shakes his head. "We been looking for that thing for three days now. Disappeared! Ask Candace."

"Candace!" he calls over his shoulder. "You seen the remote?"

A young woman joins them at the front and they unlock the latch and enter the patient area to look. "You know, I swear I saw it over here the other day . . ." The men dig between the couch cushions as Candace searches the floor underneath. "Startin' to drive me nuts, too. Wish we could just unplug it. Shoulda had like an opening for the cord or something."

After all the cushions are upended, the patients fidget and pace. The channel suddenly changes.

PANDEMONIUM

The patients scream in rage and fear as the prayers shrug off the TV loop and burn into Amelia's mind. Lucia begins wailing in Spanish at the top of her lungs, Rosemary shouts obscenities at the bewildered orderlies, and Maxwell tickles the mute viciously. The orderlies break them up to separate some into isolation rooms. Most scurry to their rooms for safety on their own.

Amelia closes her eyes with relief at the termination of the incessant praying. When she opens them, she finds the common room empty, except for the man sitting on the sofa with his back to the television. She throws the cushions back onto the other couch and sighs, looking to the man comfortably reading a newspaper with the slightest hint of a smile on his face.

"How do you deal with this place? You seem normal."

"I put myself in for medication management. Manic depression."

"You're bipolar?"

"No, I'm Marvin." He closes the newspaper to shake her hand, like a perfectly sane human being. "But I do have bipolar disorder."

Person first, of course. Why am I such an asshole?

"Amelia."

He places the paper carefully over a bump on the cushion, then leans forward, elbow to knee. "Still getting used to the place?"

"After that shitshow? Honestly, I'm just happy to be free of the Catholic channel. I don't know how you sit on that couch all day with these psychos."

"They're not psychos; they are human beings with sick brains. I am one of them. You are one of them. You're in for trying to kill yourself, right? Even Maxwell wouldn't do that."

Amelia is caught off guard. *Slash out the eyes! Break the glass and put the shards IN · · · Put them IN the corneas!* "You can't hurt yourself here, so that's a positive. Might as well try to relax, to appreciate this place for what it is: safe." *Snort shards of glass into my brain and shred it to pieces.* "I also need a safe place to go when things go sideways." Amelia considers the practicality of his glasses. *Exploding shards in the eye · · · IN the cornea.* He is safe from that.

"So you're here by choice?"

"Absolutely. It's my responsibility to myself and my loved ones to take control in my treatment, by taking my medication. I must be constantly vigilant, always on the lookout for instability. When I have big med changes, I put myself in the hospital with people who know how to help me, instead of making impossible demands on my family. It causes less dis—"

Amelia interrupts him. "Sweet! *Price Is Right*."

Marvin goes back to reading his newspaper while Amelia zones out on the well-protected TV.

LAKE OF FIRE

Everyone sits in a circle headed by a pretty nurse. The room is too warm and the plastic chairs are sticky on her naked thighs. *Pull out the eyes and put them in expensive liquor.*

"Welcome, everyone. Please sit down, Maxwell. Good sitting!" What am I, eight? "For our new faces, I'm Nurse Jessica, and I'm happy to be here with you today." Amelia's brain offers up another Rodgers and Hammerstein song. "Let's open with a prayer. Please hold hands."

Everybody joins hands except for Amelia, who doesn't move. Siamese children are rustling in the nurse's skirts; bustle full and hoops tripping little feet. The patients stare at her and prod her with elbows. When she refuses to join hands, Lucia begins praying while trying to drape her rosary over Amelia's head.

"Padre nuestro, que estás en el cielo. Santificado sea tu nombre. Venga tu reino," begins the woman. *Flay the innocent. Wear the crown. Bloody, broken man · · · Betrayed man. If your eye causeth you to sin, pluck it out; if your hand causeth you to sin, cut it off.*

"I'd really rather not. Please stop." *Pluck it out.* "No, I don't want that." *Cut it off.*

"Hágase tu voluntad en la tierra como en el cielo!" *Strips of skin · · · GUILTY!* screams the archangel. *Peel off His skin and cast your lots.*

"No. Thank you, no."

Sinner . . . hisses the serpent.

The woman is intent on forcing Amelia to wear the beads, and she prays louder.

"*Danos hoy nuestro pan de cada día.*" Crown of thorns. *Crown of shit.*

"Please stop."

He begged for mercy and You BETRAYED Him! You betrayed us · · · The both of us · · ·

"*Perdona nuestras ofensas, como también nosotros perdonamos a los que nos ofenden—*" Tear out the eyes! *TEAR OUT THE EYES! Pluck them out! Cut it off! Kill it! Kill it! Kill it! Kill it!*

"No! I don't want that!" Lucia successfully gets the rosary around Amelia's neck. Rage roars in her head. Amelia sees stars. "WHAT IS THIS?!" She twists the rosary tight around her neck and jerks it up like a noose. The rosary snaps and Lucia crosses herself. "I can't even HANG myself with this! What is it good for? Nothing! There's nothing you can say that can convince me that there is a loving, forgiving god." The woman's screeching infects Amelia's brain like bleach fumes. *Cut out the eyes.* "I don't know what you're saying!" *Plank in your eye.* "I don't know what you're saying. Speak fucking English!" Amelia throws the destroyed rosary on the floor, and Lucia picks it up, shouting in Spanish.

"*Gloria al Padre, al Hijo y al Espíritu Santo!*" The theme song to a Spanish educational program they showed in Amelia's elementary school in 1992 begins in her head, drowning out Lucia's prayers. "*Como era en el principio!*" *Whip the sinner-puppets.* "*Ahora y siempre!*" The puppets sing a greeting in Spanish. "*Por los siglos de los siglos!*" Little white children respond. The song bores into her skull. "*Amén.* AMEN!" A female orderly appears and sweeps Lucia out of the room.

Amelia stands on the edge of the group, livid, enveloped in static. Christ is bloodied and broken in her mind · · · A wasted corpse in a heap. Scapegoat. There is a tense silence, until Rosemary reaches across her empty seat, sealing her out of the circle.

"Let her go to Hell. She deserves it."

Nurse Jessica agrees but disapproves. "That is not the way to win souls."

"Yeah, and fuck your Hell cuz if I fucking go to her Hell I'm gonna fucking fuck her and him, too!" points out Maxwell.

"Please come sit," the pretty nurse gestures to the empty chair. Amelia sits. I will not make you my scapegoat. No moral person would accept the sacrifice of an innocent life to avoid the consequences of their own behavior. "You will receive no penalty for not participating in group prayer, but I do hope you continue to pray on your own. The rest of you may bow your heads." Everyone bows their heads. Amelia drowns out the sound of their babbling with Nirvana. Every patient opens their eyes at some point to peek at her.

"Amen," the group mumbles. They squeeze hands and settle in their chairs. The out-of-tune guitar twangs in Amelia's head.

"Today, we are talking about being proactive. Does anyone know what 'proactive' means?" asks the nurse.

Maxwell balances his chair on its two back legs and says, "Pedro, you need to get some of that zit shit. Proactiv." Nurse Jessica ignores him and answers her own question.

"Being proactive is taking responsibility in ensuring a better outcome in your treatment." Amelia is amused by the song. "What do you do to be proactive, Marvin?"

"Well, I'm here. I put myself in here looking for help, so I think that's pretty proactive," he replies.

"It certainly is! What about you, Pedro?" she asks the plain, bulky teen.

"Umm . . . take my medicine?"

She nods to him. "Very good." Amelia is next in the circle. "How about you?" The music skips.

"What?"

"What do you do to be proactive . . . ?" The nurse doesn't know her name.

"Amelia."

"Amelia. How do you take responsibility in your treatment?"

"What do I do to be proactive?" *If your eye causeth you to sin, pluck it out; if your hand causeth you to sin, cut it off.* "Die. Try to die. That's the only way it ends. This suicide . . . it made me feel like I had some control over it. Like I really tried to do something about my condition." *Pluck it out. Cut it off.* "The people who want me to self-medicate don't want me to do what makes THEM feel uncomfortable. They want me to pray, go for a jog, drink a cup of tea or something, go pet puppies at the mall, as if that would relieve my craving to cut off my feet and pop my eyeballs like big empty gumballs that split open exactly as I imagine my eyes would. I resent that." *Pluck it out.* "If nothing can heal me—not love or God or myself—then it certainly seems that I'm going to be this way indefinitely. Possibly forever. And I cannot handle that. I can barely stand being this way for an afternoon. Imagine a lifetime." *Cut it off.* "Could you constantly live with something you hate as much as I hate myself? Probably not." *Drown her. Drown them all.*

"Would anyone like to explain why suicide is the most selfish thing anyone can do to their loved ones?" Nurse Jessica opens the question to the group.

Rosemary looks at Amelia haughtily, and says, "It's a mortal sin. You're going to Hell for that."

"In Mark 3:29, Jesus says that the only unforgivable sin is denial of the Holy Spirit." *I DENY THE HOLY SPIRIT! I DENY*

THE HOLY SPIRIT! "Everything else can be forgiven."

"What about all the people you hurt?" asks Marvin. *I DENY THE HOLY SPIRIT!*

"It's the combination of 'I want to die' and 'I'm worthless' that is so deadly. You people want to live because you love yourself so damn much; the more special you think you are, the more your friends and family will grieve over you in your imagination. You couldn't possibly do that to them; that would be SO selfish because they would miss you and cry. But when you think you're the shit under their shoes, your existence appears more like something you would be kind to rid them of." I wish I had been an abortion.

Maxwell points at Amelia. "Selfish! You're a selfish bitch!"

"Eyes to me," Nurse Jessica lightly snaps her fingers. "Charlie, what do you do to be proactive?" The song stops as Charlie takes a deep breath and looks up at the ceiling. *Jack-in-the-box.*

"Showers. I take showers. They remind me of the boundaries of my body, where I end and the world begins. The sensation of hot water on my skin, it just brings me back."

"I do that when I'm too drunk to stand: sit on the shower floor til I'm sober," quips Maxwell.

A dozen drunken showers flash through Amelia's head. Great. I have something in common with that psycho.

"In what other ways is a shower beneficial?" asks the pretty nurse.

Faces in the marble. Charlie picks at the fingernails on his left hand.

"I get clean. Sometimes, I get so depressed that I can't even face washing myself. I can't handle the thought of the whole process of showering. It's overwhelming. Then, when I get in, I'm like, 'Why can't I stay in here forever?'"

Nurse Jessica nods. "And maybe there's a type of rebirth in that baptism." *Don't drown the baby.*

"Yeah, maybe," he allows, "Or a womb-related thing. I don't know." *What are they doing to the baby?*

"Very nice." The nurse is pleased. *They're drowning it.* "Thank you for a productive discussion." Slaves sing a lullaby between Amelia's ears. "Rosemary, what do you do to be proactive?"

"I don't even know what that means," sniffs the old woman. "Is it SEXUAL?"

With mastered coolness, Nurse Jessica explains, "Not at all. It means doing something to take control of your treatment. What makes you feel better when you're down?"

"I wash my vagina. Or that nigger girl does it for me." *She said it again!* shrieks a kindergartener.

"So, also washing." Nurse Jessica deflects the question to the man balancing precariously on his chair. "Maxwell?"

"I drink. And take drugs . . . lots of drugs." He eye-fucks the nurse and mouth-rapes her with his words. "Fucking hookers is also good. That makes me feel REAL nice."

Nurse Jessica tilts her head a thread of a degree. "Something productive please."

Maxwell barks a laugh and slams the front legs of his chair back onto the floor. "Productive like sitting on the floor of the shower, or hacking my arms to bits, or washing my junk? That kind of proactive productive production?" The pink lips of his inner eyes curl toward his eyebrows as he catches a new target. The third eyelid flashes again. "I want to know what John Doe here does to be proactive." He stands up and looms menacingly over a tall young man sitting rigidly on the edge of the group. His eyes are glazed over. *Is he lucky that he can't function?* "Mr. Doe, do you have any hobbies that distract you from being a grade-A psychopath? Gardening perhaps? What makes you feel better about getting an injection straight into your temple twice daily?" Or trapped inside there somewhere, screaming to be let out? "Hello? Anybody in there?"

Nurse Jessica keeps her face impassive. "Maxwell, if you would like to be excused for the remainder of the session, you may be, but please use your words instead of actions."

"Only if you chart me for it. Incident report!" He starts slapping his hands together like violent sex, grinding against the man's chair and making grunting noises. "Incident report! Incident report!"

Daniel comes over and Max immediately puts his hands in the air. Testicle tourniquet. He turns on his heel. "Goodbye, Max!" bids the pretty nurse with a smile. X-acto knife. "I think we need a change of tone. Think hard. Amelia, would you like to make any additions from earlier? About being proactive?"

Amelia searches her brain. *Go with the program,* urged Jason, who sodomized her wounds with his forceps and cared for her. Get out. Die on your own terms. "Yes. Music."

"Yes!" Nurse Jessica just won the lowest-value carnival prize. "Music can be a wonderful tool in managing your symptoms. Many people find relief in it, myself included." A diatribe about the psychological attributes of **D minor** runs in Amelia's mind, but she says nothing. "That is a very positive addition. Thank you for your participation. Please, all of you, take the rest of the session off. Use the time to do something proactive."

THE JACKOFF

Amelia sits alone playing solitaire after lunch while Charlie smokes. *Judge Judy* blares in the background, drowning out any chance of musical escape. The disembodied hands are typing. *For the generations to come, none of your descendants who has a defect may come to offer the food of his God. No man who has any defect of mind or body may come near: No man who is blind or lame, disfigured or deformed; no man with a crippled foot or hand, or who is hunchbacked or dwarfed, or who has any eye defect, or who has festering or running sores or damaged testicles. Because of his defect, he must not go near the curtain or approach the altar, and so desecrate my sanctuary.* She squeezes her eyes shut. I am about to scream. I am going to scream.

"Excuse me."

Amelia looks up to see a young man shadowed by Daniel. He smells dangerous. Look at how close Daniel is. "What."

The young man has pasty skin and no shame. "I was wondering if you would have sex with me."

What the fuck?

"No."

"Why not?" he says, throwing up his hands in exasperation.

"I don't find you attractive."

"You don't get to judge me. You don't even know my name!"

She inhales through her tear ducts and rolls her dry eyes in their sockets. "It's a little late for that."

"It's Jack," he announces proudly. "Jack OFF."

"No fucking way."

"Look, lady—" His body language becomes agitated. "—I have a perfectly average penis. Perfectly average. It's as thick as my thumb and four and a half inches long, just let me show it to you." Jackoff displays his penis with showmanship. Daniel hastily steps closer to him. Amelia wants to hurt and humiliate him.

"That's fucking small."

"It is not!" he screams. "It's perfectly average! You didn't see it up close!" His mouth becomes a sardonic grimace and he lunges at Amelia. "You're going to fuck me!" *Rape the shit slut fat fuck · · · Tear open the pussy and make her bleed. Infect her with your seed and kill it in the womb.*

Daniel instantly steps in and restrains the young man. As he wrestles him away from her, Jackoff glares at Amelia and threatens to beat her to death if she doesn't fuck him.

I'd kill it in the womb, she decides.

UNTO US

In the brightly decorated art therapy room, Amelia is using a special paintbrush with which she cannot hurt herself. She paints black and red robots on everything they give her, and is immersed in Handel's "Messiah." "For Unto Us a Child is Born" breaks over her mind in waves. **For unto us a child is** · · · **For unto us a child is** · · · The sopranos begin the runs at measure ten. The vocal acrobatics it takes to sing this piece of music cause the muscles around her larynx to contract and change shape just as if she were singing out loud, as she has done every Christmas since middle school. Strings! Lift the left palm.

Amelia conducts the choir in her mind. Maxwell jumps up in his chair and raises his hand.

"Hey you! Fat! This bitchfreak isn't following directions! She's got robots everywhere. Not following directions. That is not a 'soul rainbow!'"

Amelia focuses on the pincer-claws of her current painting and the song at measure twenty-two. **And the GovernMent shall Be upOn his Shoul—** It's clever here; enter soprano, bass, and tenor. The fat therapist waddles toward Amelia.

"Don't you remember how we talked about the soul rainbow?" **And His name shall be call-ed** "And how each color represents something unique to you?"

Wonderful! "I'm doing robots." **Counselor!**

"Well I guess it doesn't really matter cuz there's only five more minutes anyway." The fat lady squishes her shoulders into her ears and shrugs. **The Mighty God!** "Let's clean up, everyone!" she calls to the room. **The Everlasting Father!** "Put your paintings on the piano to dry; we'll talk about them on Friday." **The Prince of Peace.**

Her fingers itching to tap out the simple but hearty accompaniment, Amelia pauses at the piano with the painting in her hand **And the GovernMent shall Be upOn his Shoul—** She is close enough to smell the strings. **And the GovernMent shall Be upOn his Shoul—der.**

"Is it alright if I play something?"

"This is ART therapy," says the fat therapist. **And His name shall be call-ed** "If you want music therapy you're out of luck." **Wonderful!** The piano is calling to her with echoes of wit and pain.

"Are you saying that music isn't art?" **Counselor!** The accompaniment hops in her head, upright and clean. **The Mighty God!**

"I'm saying you have no idea how crazy things get if I open that piano." **The Everlasting Father!** "Every patient wants a turn banging on it—" **The Prince of Peace.** "—and then it's MY ass in trouble with the doctors."

Amelia gives the fat therapist her paper covered in robots and follows the song out of the room.

MIRRORS IN THE MIRROR

Amelia is waiting as the common room fills up with visitors. "Spiegel im Spiegel" tiptoes through her mind. I've always been fond of 6/4. She can see the sheet music. Daddy loved it when I played Arvo Pärt. She glimpses her father signing in. The violin enters with him. They awkwardly stop in front of each other. The piano booms.

"I'm so sorry, Daddy." Amelia's father tries not to look at her bandages.

"I'm just glad you're alive. Thank God you called 911."

They sit down at a card table and the piano booms again. She can't look him in the eye. Amelia breaks through the barrier of the song. "How's Mom taking it?" The violin purrs a slow melody, while the rhythm continues in her head.

"Not well. Alexis is defending you tooth and nail," he starts.

"Defending me? For what?" *SINNER.*

"Being selfish." *You fucking piece of shit stupid, selfish bitch.* "According to them. I don't think you're selfish. I know you've suffered for a long time, and I'm sorry we didn't get you help sooner."

"You did the best you could."

"Alexis keeps trying to explain chemical imbalances to Mom and Andrew, but you know how it is . . . We don't believe in medication." She screamed. "Mom thinks you're not trying hard enough to be positive, and your brother is furious that you did it two days after his birthday." Andrew teaching her how to climb a tree · · · Building a fort in the woods · · · Giving her her first beer.

The guilt is crushing.

"I'm sorry, I couldn't wait any longer. I was planning for the first of May, I just couldn't stand it anymore. I had to! It's unbearable!"

"You don't have to defend yourself to me. You might not want to call home anytime soon, though. They're not ready to talk to you. I never thought your sister would be your biggest champion, but she's the one helping them process it." *Stupid, selfish, ratshit-infested psycho.*

"Well please thank her for me."

"I will," her father promises. He looks at the table. "Have you talked to Chris?"

"Yeah. He called off the wedding." She rubs her eyes. "Said he never wants to see my face again."

"I'd expect nothing more. Is he at least coming up from Florida to see you?" She puts her head in her hands.

"Definitely not. His dad is dying, so he doesn't want to leave his side, which I totally understand." The song soothes her. "I wouldn't want him here, anyway. There's nothing to say that hasn't been said before." There is a long pause while the violin climbs the staff.

"We should have gotten you help sooner. We shouldn't have left you to the counselors at church. When you were in high school, we thought it would be just a phase—" The last chorus of "Just a Phase" by Incubus suddenly bursts into Amelia's head. It is so loud that she has trouble hearing the rest of the conversation. "I just didn't know what to do. I thought you'd grow out of it. We thought it'd go away." The song is at its apex. "You've been so much happier since you started college, and now you do this months before you graduate?"

"Killing myself before I graduate and get married is just a manifestation of how truly hopeless I am." The music crescendos and Boyd makes heart-wrenching noises. The open fifths are filling up with every repetition, all the way to her bones. "This is the only way I can be free of it: to die. I want to be dead. I wish I were dead.

I'm sorry, but that's the truth: I wish I were dead." She watches Mike Einziger squeeze the guitar strings in her head.

"Well, I'm glad you're not. We're all glad that you're okay."

"I'm not okay," she says reflexively.

"Safe, then," he amends. "We're glad you're safe and getting the help you need."

"I love you, Daddy." She hangs her head as the song deflates. "I'm so sorry."

"I love you, too, sweetheart," he says, and it comforts her.

THE REAL SOLUTION

The sun is coming up, and Amelia is wide awake. In order to distract her from visions of decomposing heads being sewn onto new bodies, she keeps her eyes open and listens to "Real Solution #9" by White Zombie. A good Christian lady speaks sternly to her from a pulpit. Would this be considered a recitative? Lucia begins her morning prayers in Spanish at the top of her lungs. The ward starts to wake up. Rosemary needs to wash her vagina. Amelia has been waiting for an orderly to give her permission to escape her confinement. The door opens halfway.

"Out of bed, Amelia," a woman says, and disappears.

She trudges to the common room where Charlie and Marvin already occupy a table.

"Could not fucking sleep last night. Charlie? Marvin? Do you hear this bitch across the ward?" She plops down in a chair.

"Who, Rosemary? Was she at it again?"

"Not her. The religious Mexican," Amelia starts. "Lucia? The one who tried to make me wear the rosary, screaming I don't know what for two hours straight last night, and then again this morning."

"Yeah, she does that," Marvin shrugs.

"Yes, and it's driving me crazy. At least scream in English so I can come up with some clever arguments to entertain myself. She's always railing at me in Spanish, and it's so disrespectful to come to a country and not learn the language. I fucking hate Spanish; it's my second least-favorite language."

"Well, think of who you're dealing with, here," says Marvin.

"This is a woman who screams, and she just happens to scream in Spanish. If she were from Germany, she'd be screaming in German. She is mentally ill."

Amelia is irritated by his logic, but Charlie breaks the standoff.

"Marvin? Don't be offended when I say this, but, I've been meaning to ask . . . Are African American women's vaginas . . . really purple?"

Marvin laughs, but Amelia is ensconced in the song again. "Everyone is different. There is sort of a general standard, and then there are exceptions. And those exceptions can be . . . differently pigmented," he explains.

Maxwell barges into their conversation, already holding three cups of coffee. "Who wants to give me coffeeeeee?"

Marvin speaks without looking at the man. "I'm sorry, but we're all drinking our coffee." Maxwell goes immediately to the next table without comment.

Charlie makes a face and says, "At least you don't have to deal with THAT nutcase in your ward. When he gets going, he just never. shuts. the fuck. up."

"It's just, I haven't slept more than three hours at a time for almost a month," Amelia slumps in her chair. "I don't know how I'm functioning. I just can never get to sleep. My mind won't turn off." She grimaces. "And the nightmares . . ."

"Bad?" asks Charlie.

"GRUESOME. Last night I dreamed a witch was pulling out my intestines and turning them on a spit, but like, slowly." Lying on a table, strapped down, abdomen sliced open. Wrap the intestines around and turn turn turn. It made a sticky, glopping sound.

"That explains your bad mood," Marvin says, knowingly.

His presumption irritates her.

"That one single dream . . . OR my general desperate desire to see Death's maggot-ridden grin." *Take me into your arms and infect me with your pus.*

"And that," he concedes.

"Yes, that," says Charlie. "What IS that? I've never heard anyone talk about being suicidal, and it's SO interesting, and SO fucked up. 'Death's maggot-ridden mouth'?"

"Grin," she corrects him. *Chew off my face.*

He backs off a little, but still asks, "Did something bad happen to you?"

"No. And I think that makes it worse because I have nothing to blame it on."

"So, you just . . . want to die."

He does not understand.

"No, I want to kill myself."

"If there a difference?"

"Yes." Amelia becomes still. "Suicide is more . . . empowering. Waiting to die, well, that's more passive, and you have no time guarantee on that."

"You don't want to die an old lady, in your sleep?" Marvin inquires.

"I'm already dead."

BETTER THAN YOURS

"Milkshake" by Kelis loops in Amelia's head as she steps in rhythm into the registered psychiatric nurse's office. Fuck this stupid song. She knocks lightly on the half-open door. "I'm Amelia. I'm supposed to come at one thirty?"

The woman is leaning back in her chair with her ankle on the top of her thigh. She makes a minute gesture with the very tip of her left index finger, toward the chair. "Yes, please sit down." The RPN does not stand up to shake Amelia's hand. "I have some questions and some answers for you," says the statue.

"Alright." Amelia sits. Fuck this fucking SONG!

"Are you currently in a state where you have more energy than usual?"

Amelia pushes through the repetition to speak. "I'm not sleeping, so it's hard to tell. There is a point where insomnia becomes so bad that interacting with others is simply a series of flashing colors, lights, and sounds with a sum total of 'good' or 'bad' when it's over. But I don't remember a single individual goddamn word."

The RPN nods, bored or indifferent. "Do you ever see things that maybe aren't real?"

"Maggots. Crows. People lurking in corners. Bicyclists swerving into my car when I'm driving." Amelia tries to shake off the song, but the earworm is buried deep. "The real problem is the music. It never shuts off. Sometimes it's so loud that I can't hear myself think. The worst is when I only know a short portion of a piece, and it plays over and over and over again. I get these awful loops stuck in my head, and the only way to fight that is to hum the theme to *I Dream of Jeannie.* *Don't be a weirdo and fucking do that in front of her* · · · I'm not! Jesus! "I don't know why that works, but it's a fucking lifesaver." She thinks of the *I Dream of Jeannie* song, but doesn't hum it out loud. A brief moment of silence before Kelis starts again.

The nameless nurse's toes twitch, and she asks, "Do you ever think about other things that later make no sense?"

"Yeah, that's why I stopped drinking bottled water. Unless I could see it coming from the tap, I KNEW it was lighter fluid. It was so stupid but I couldn't bring myself to drink it and risk having my lungs set on fire."

"Very interesting," the woman perks up subtly at this addition. "Okay, how have you acted toward others, recently?"

"I've been a bad friend. Angry and irritable and reckless. And mean. There is nothing left in me to give to anyone who claims to care about me. I guess that's why I quarantine myself when I get like this."

"Quarantine," repeats the nurse. "That's a strong word."

"Not strong enough for what I deserve."

"Do you often go into a depression after these episodes?"

"Every day is just varying degrees of suicidal. Each depth of depression has its own nuances." Fuck you brain. Fuck you Kelis. Fuck this crazy shit. I am DONE. I'm DONE.

"Are you experiencing any good feelings right now, like euphoria or extreme joy?"

"I can't even remember joy." The song digs deeper into Amelia's eardrums like a hot corkscrew, tapeworms embedded in her most sensitive parts. "I just want to die."

"You're having suicidal thoughts right now?" asks the nurse.

"Yes. On the good days, I don't want to live. Then I want to die. Then I want someone to kill me. Then I want to kill myself. In that order. And it's been that way for a decade."

"So," the RPN uncrosses her legs, "suicide ideation since puberty. Even when you have a lot of energy?"

"Desperation," Amelia growls through clenched teeth. I want a new song NOW! Fucking RIGHT NOW you stupid fucking assholes! The disembodied hands hesitate, then type: *M-i-l-k-s-h-a-k-e.*

"And would you say you spend more of your time depressed or agitated?" Oh, fuck you. Very funny. So fucking clever.

"Depressed. Though the two are not mutually exclusive."

"I see." Now, only the word 'milkshake' repeats itself incessantly. "Thank you for sharing this information with me; it will help us properly diagnose you." The RPN pulls out a prescription pad. "First, we have to get you sleeping. I'm prescribing Trazodone. It will help you sleep. You cannot abuse it or get high on it because it puts you out in fifteen minutes. Possible side effects include"—the song pauses when it registers with Amelia that she is going to be taking a pill—"nausea, vomiting, dizziness, headache, fainting, and in some cases seizures. Here is the pamphlet. You will begin taking it this evening at 9 p.m. med call."

"Okay . . ." ::SILENCE:: "You said you had answers?"

"Yes," replies the RPN. "The question is sleep and the answer is Trazodone." The stupid fucking song starts over from the chorus. "You'll get to see Dr. Stephens on Monday, and you can address any of your concerns then. Anything else?"

"I guess not."

"Excellent. Have an excellent day."

THE CASUAL ANOREXIC

Charlie and Amelia sit facing each other at a card table, waiting for their meals to be served. "Amazing Grace" has been on a continuous loop in her head for the last two hours. As an orderly places a tray in front of Amelia, her stomach gives a lurch. *Jack-in-the-box. Ewww,* the kindergarteners complain. This is a standard hospital meal, she explains to them. Meat, starch, vegetables. Amelia imagines maggots writhing in the meat. Potatoes are seared flaccid penises. Peas are poisonous berries.

Charlie digs in. "I have a love/hate relationship with Salisbury steak," he says around a mouthful of pig shit half-hardened in the sun. "It's so good, and as long as I chew every bite twenty-five times it's really easy to purge."

"Why twenty-five?" asks Amelia.

"It tricks my mind into thinking I'm eating more than I actually am, and it mashes the food so fine that it comes right up."

"But why twenty-five? Is that number special to you?"

"What? No. How can a number be special? I read it on a ProAna message board a few months ago." He loads another bite into his mouth.

"Right on," she says, attempting to cut a potato with the side of her spork. *Jack-in-the-box.*

Charlie cocks his head to the side and swallows. "So, I've been dying to ask . . . What's with you? You're obviously not that thin naturally, your shoulders are too wide. Restrict? Purge? Both?" *STARVE THE DUMB WHORE FAT FUCK.*

"I try to not obsess about it. I'm a casual anorexic. Yogurt and diet ginger ale. Too busy to eat. Kill myself a little more every day. It's excruciating, but no more so than existing and not doing anything to alleviate my condition." Amelia uses the prongs of her utensil to carefully stab the potato skin down the middle. *It doesn't need to eat,* rasps a voice in her head. "Until recently, I was only starving myself recreationally. I don't meet the diagnostic criteria for anorexia, but I do try to eat fewer than eight hundred calories a day."

"I could never . . ." Charlie looks at her, eyes shining, and sighs. "I don't have the willpower for that. Don't you get hungry?" He starts in on the potatoes.

She scoops the white fluff out of the brown starch. Buddha lived on one mustard seed a day for seven years. "Honestly, I fucking hate food. I get absolutely no pleasure from it. Eating is a chore and I only do it so I don't pass out."

"What, like, it doesn't taste good?" Charlie asks, confused.

"It doesn't taste like anything. Imagine forcing yourself to swallow a mouthful of sawdust." *Jack-in-the-box.* "Take away the taste of something, and it completely changes the experience of eating. That shit you're eating would be lukewarm Styrofoam in my mouth. A fresh peach is biting into a cold, runny, half-boiled egg. Chocolate milk is snot, and red wine is the puddle that collects under wet garbage in a dumpster. All textures and fluids are indistinguishable from one another."

"You binge, though," he says with a conspiratorial smile. "Everybody binges. What happens after you binge? Do you deal with it?" *Jack-in-the-box.* "Or do you hate yourself for it?"

"I guess I don't feel bad when I eat too much because it's not about being skinny, it's about being dead. If I eat too much, that's just that much longer I have to wait."

"You're purposefully trying to die from starvation?" asks Charlie. Amelia looks at him pointedly as he swallows.

"Anorexia and cigarettes are the only socially acceptable forms of suicide."

"But not bulimia?" *HYPOCRITE!*

"Honestly, no, because bulimia is succumbing to weakness, then cheating your way out of it. Anorexia is being stronger than your most natural instincts. No one would ever admit it, but they're secretly impressed by anorexia. Just think of how awestruck they are by monks who do it."

Charlie shakes his head and saws at his meat with his sad, stupid, plastic utensil. "Dying is not impressive. Dying is losing the game. You gotta be light AND alive to enjoy it."

Amelia's eyes harden. "You enjoy it?" ::SILENCE:: "Your eating disorder is a billboard of your internal status. You obviously don't enjoy it. And the way you do it . . . you can't miss that. You can't 'He seemed so normal' it away when you're puking your guts up after every meal."

"I didn't mean I enjoy it," he gets defensive. "I meant like, it gives me a purpose."

This is a satisfactory answer for Amelia. She unhappily hovers her spork over the roasted potatoes, and quickly puts one in her mouth to choke down as fast as possible, like a dog swallowing a pill wrapped in cheese.

Charlie smiles. "There you go. Not so bad, right?"

It's like eating paper maché, she wants to say. It sticks in my mouth, my throat · · · Glue tumbling down my esophagus and coating my stomach like the thick white substance within a milkweed.

"It tastes like Wite-Out," she confesses.

"I have some ketchup packets stashed in my room. Maybe the

salt will help," offers Charlie.

Amelia considers this gesture. It would be impolite to refuse, but that will just make it taste like salty Wite-Out. It doesn't occur to either of them that hoarding ketchup packets is strange.

"Come on. By my count you've had about three hundred calories today. That's a good two hundred more of potatoes and peas."

Sad little dicks and American nightshade.

"All right, Charlie. Thanks."

When he gets up to go to his room, Amelia clandestinely adds three of her potatoes and two scoops of peas onto Charlie's tray. Enough to make a difference, but not enough for him to notice. *Jack-in-the-box. Jack-in-the-box. Jack-in-the-box.*

DON'T EXPECT ME TO CRY

"Let us pray," begins Nurse Jessica. The group reaches around Amelia to hold hands, and the flat, shameless chords of "Jesus Doesn't Want Me for a Sunbeam" stumble into her head. The standard grunge chords. Doesn't get much easier than that. Her soft palate lifts · · · Middle school. Kurt Cobain escaped his bondage, and they turned on the TVs like he was the president. He starts to sing. This makes her wonder why people would not suspect that someone who wrote a song called "I Hate Myself and Want to Die" was in danger of suicide. I talked about it all the time. Maybe too much. Trying to prepare them for the inevitable.

"Amen," choruses the group.

"I thought today might be a good day to address how spirituality can help you recover from your disorders," says the nurse. "Is that okay with you, Amelia?"

Amelia pauses. She's trying to convert me. "Yes. In fact, I'd like to share a Bible verse, if I may," she tells the surprised nurse.

"Well that sounds lovely. Do you need to borrow my Bible?"

"Actually, could you read it out loud for me? I get nervous." Nurse Jessica pulls the book off the shelf with a smug look. "It's Matthew 6:5–6," says Amelia.

The nurse flips to the Gospels, finds the page, then begins to read. "'Whenever you pray, do not be like the hypocrites; for they love to stand and pray in the synagogues and at the street corners, so that they may be seen by others.'" She pauses, casts a wary eye to Amelia, then continues. "'But whenever you pray, go into your closet and shut the door and pray to your Father in secret; and your Father who sees in secret will reward you.'"

Amelia smirks as the nurse snaps the Bible shut. The nurse composes herself, and addresses the rest of the group as if nothing was said. "Who wants to start?"

Pedro raises his hand. Nurse Jessica gives him an award-winning smile, and he begins meekly. "Going to church is the closest I get to like I was before, you know, the medicine and stuff. I get that feeling of having someone there for me, and it's like, good, I think. And when they lay their hands on me, I know that if I just believed enough, I would be healed. And that gives me hope."

Nurse Jessica beams. "Thank you, Pedro. Would anyone like to comment?" It's clear that the nurse has an agenda, so Amelia pipes up again.

"I'm sorry, Pedro, but that is just bullshit. Jesus doesn't 'want you for a sunbeam.' We will never be good enough to deserve healing. WE," she gestures around the circle, "will never be worthy of His affection. Only 144,000 people are getting into Heaven anyway, and they all have to be descendants of the twelve tribes of Israel. What makes you think we're so special?"

"By their fruit they shall be known," Rosemary regurgitates at random. "Maybe you should read the WHOLE Bible before you say nasty things about your Creator."

"I've read the entire Bible twice," Amelia retorts. "Your loving god destroyed me and left me clutching ashes." The crow bobs its head in agreement. "That god has forsaken me. And you. Betrayed you." She looks at Pedro. "You know people who have been healed, right? Why them and not you? How could God relieve them of their pain, and ignore you? 'Ask and you shall receive?' I asked. Begged. They want you to beg, and He refused." *This isn't about you, it's about him*, thinks the (usually quiet) man from Picasso's Blue Period. You're right. You're right. Sorry.

"Did they tell you, 'Give it to God, He'll take anything?'" she asks him, as the out-of-tune instruments continue in their simple pattern.

Pedro nods.

"And did you give it to Him?"

"I tried."

"How long ago?"

"Every Sunday."

Amelia shakes her head. "That is not the fair and just god that I've been told about." She leans toward him. "God does not save anyone. Tell me that Christ did not realize this when he cried out his last words, 'Why have You forsaken me?' And there was nothing. Just like there was always nothing."

"So, what, you don't believe in God but you're mad at Him?" asks Marvin.

"I don't know if God is real or not, but it makes me sad that this man, this good man, WASTED his life. For nothing. That's what's so humiliating about Jesus. He believed with his whole being, and he was wrong. He was abandoned." *Eloi, Eloi, lama sabachthani?* "You people cannot bear the thought of insignificance, so you inflate yourself with words and pictures of love after death and it is all refuse. You're standing in piles of shit, piles upon piles of shit, as I stand in and am a part of it. Only, I am looking AT it, and you are looking up, away. And I want to be swallowed up by it."

Maxwell looks up from picking at a hangnail to say, "This bitch is crazy." Amelia can feel the frequencies change as fingers drag across warped strings.

Pedro looks concerned. "What if you died and went to Hell?" *I DENY THE HOLY SPIRIT!*

89

"Then I'll deserve it, won't I? At least I'll be responsible for my own actions." She widens her focus to the entire room. "You don't think that accepting the blood of a scapegoat is morally reprehensible?"

"Amelia," Nurse Jessica steps in. "Try to look beyond your own anger. What good can come of thinking like that? That negativity is bad for us all. What will you tell your children?"

"If I stay alive long enough to have children, I will quote Epicurus to them: 'Is God willing to prevent evil, but not able? Then he is not omnipotent. Is he able, but not willing? Then he is malevolent. Is he both able and willing? Then he is responsible for evil. Is he neither able nor willing? Then why call him God?'"

"What do you think happens when we die?" asks Marvin.

"The end of consciousness. We go out like a flame. Ashes to ashes, dust to dust." The song changes into applause. Must have been the *MTV Unplugged* version. **Amazing grace /** Not this again.

"But what about the second law of thermodynamics?" Marvin asks, adjusting his glasses. "It says you can't create or destroy energy." The Earth isn't a closed system, she thinks. **How sweet the sound /** Marvin continues, "Here's a fact for you: the body weighs approximately three grams less, immediately after death. The soul has worth. And weight." **That saved a wretch like me /** I used to give that exact same argument. *You should ask him if he can name any OTHER laws of thermodynamics.* Be nice.

"Energy transfers." **I once was lost /** "When you die, your energy obviously shifts from fuel into heat when you're cremated, or into the digestive processes of the bacteria consuming you." **But now am found /** "Your energy observably transfers in a nonconscious manner to other forms." **Was blind /** "As for your 'scientific fact,' the body eliminates all waste in the bowel and bladder after death. It's not a 'soul,' it's shit." **But now I see.**

"So, like, not even a soul?" asks Charlie, surprised.

"No, not even that. Thankfully not that." **Twas grace that taught my heart to fear /** Charlie looks at her quizzically. "Thankfully, because I want to die so completely that the thought of any part of me still existing is intolerable." **And grace my fears relieved /** "If God existed, He would have cared enough to strike me down." **How precious did that grace appear /** Pedro raises his hand.

"Maybe you don't have a soul. Maybe there are other types of spirits. I don't know whether or not animals have souls, but they definitely have little spirits, little personalities." **The hour I first believed.** "So there are puppy spirits, and human spirits, and spirits for people like you. And God just hates it."

Maxwell clacks his chair legs on the linoleum and attacks without warning, "What would you know about it, you pussy ass faggot? Can't even sleep without the lights on. Have you seen this guy? Strapped to a gurney in the hallway under the emergency lights all night?" **Through many dangers, toils, and snares /**

"Fuck off, asshole," replies Pedro.

"Why do you sleep in the hall?" Amelia asks the young man. **I have already come /**

"When the lights are out, I see little green creatures everywhere, and I can feel them crawling into my ears and nose." **Tis grace has brought me safe thus far /** His eyes are filled with fear. "I can see them marching up and down my body." **And grace will lead us home.** See? FUCK that god! she wants to scream, but his pain distracts her.

"Can't they just leave on the light?" **The Lord has promised good to me /**

Nurse Jessica gives a response straight from the book. "Policy is that lights in individual rooms go off at ten o'clock. No exceptions."

His word my hope secures /

"But that's stupid!" bursts out Amelia. "Why can't they just leave the lights on?" **He will my shield and portion be /** She questions Jessica directly. "If it helps him, why can't you just leave the lights on?" The voices in the room and in her head are murmuring assent. **As long as life endures.**

The nurse snaps her fingers and the song stops. "We are not here to discuss Pedro's sleeping issues. We are here to witness to someone in need of . . . support." She means 'Salvation.' I can almost hear those words coming out of my mouth five years ago. "Now, if there are no further direct questions for Amelia, we will continue around the circle and each tell a story of how faith got us through a hard time. Uninterrupted."

CIGARETTES AND
CHOCOLATE MILK

Amelia squints in the haze of the smoking lounge, accompanied by a song by Rufus Wainwright. "I can't believe you dragged me in here, Charlie."

"It's wonderful, isn't it?" He takes a deep breath and smiles. "Take it all in."

"No. I think I already have emphysema," she says with a wrinkled nose. "And I definitely reek like an ashtray. Gross, man."

The tar rabbit perks up its ears.

Charlie produces a cigarette and the lighter he checked out at the desk in the hall. "You know, it's the funniest thing to me that you say you're so committed to death, but then you won't even try a cigarette because of the health complications. Too funny." The song turns minor.

"Sorry if I don't want my hair to fall out from chemo, or hack up black tar from my lungs every fifteen minutes. It's just one of the ugliest deaths available." The Lenox figurine takes off her scarf to reveal a bald head. Now can you love me? "I guess every cigarette is a death threat, which has a kind of drama to it, if you're into that."

Charlie lights the tip and puffs. "You still want to die, don't you?"

"Of course I do, cigarettes would just take too long. I don't know if I can stay alive that long," she says. Charlie takes a drag and performs a French inhale. The tar rabbit approves. "How can you stand that horrible shit? It's fucking disgusting. You smell like a bowling alley."

"Keeps me thin," he smacks his lips. "Lower chance of bingeing."

"I'm willing to go to great lengths to be thin, but not subject myself to this noxious shit." *Jack-in-the-box.* She crosses her arms. "Why do you binge and purge? I feel like that's cheating. You deserve to get fat from those calories. You need to own your choices, and let the scale be the judge."

"Fuck you, I like eating, I just don't like being fat," he exhales on a long stream of smoke. Amelia judges him straight to his face.

"Well it's like you don't have any self-control."

"That's the problem: I don't. This food thing . . . I've completely lost control. It's taken over my life, and now I'm having heart problems . . . one of my teeth came out . . ." He ashes on the floor, embarrassed. "That's why my parents put me in here. I can't even function. My life has come to a complete stop."

His clown hides deeper than mine. She wonders how deep that box is. "That's crazy. Your tooth fell out?" He nods but doesn't look at her. "And you're at Northwestern?"

Charlie takes another drag. "I just took a leave of absence. I'm on the wrestling team, and this kind of thing is common in that sport."

"I have a full academic scholarship, and failed this semester." Don't throw the desk at the teacher. He can look at her again.

"You just have to talk to them. They were very accommodating." Don't throw the desk at the teacher.

"Have you chosen a major?" she pries.

"Still undecided. You?"

"Psychology, if you can believe it." STEREOTYPE. "It's like I was in such agony, I thought that if I studied it, I could find

out how to fix myself. I pored through journals and read all kinds
of research, but none of it fits me quite right." Amelia's brain flips
through hundreds of pages of books while the bridge trips along her
consciousness, until she finds *DSM-IV* diagnostic criteria. Schizo-
phrenia. Schizoaffective. Bipolar disorder. Borderline personality disorder. Major depressive episode. "I just want to die ALL the time,
and I don't know if I can be fixed. It's beyond the reach of my coping
skills." The tar rabbit sniffs the air, its snout black and wet. "So I burn
myself to make the numbness go away. I can't control my emotional
pain so I manifest it into something I can treat. Only on the right side
of my stomach—the evil side. Always hidden, not like those fucking
idiots who hack up their arms and thighs where everyone can see their
weakness." The piano peals.

"Why would you hurt yourself without trying to die?"

*If you eye causeth you to sin, pluck it out. If your hand causeth
you to sin, cut it off.*

"At first, I wanted to show God that I was willing to sacrifice
my flesh, as His son did. That I TRULY repented of my sins, so
He would heal me of this affliction." The piano solo builds, full of
imperfections from a sound check before a concert she went to see
with her friends in 2003. "Like I said, hidden. Secret. A contract
between me and God."

"And you weren't healed," he says in a cloud.

"No."

"And did you keep doing it when you lost your faith?"

"Yes," she admits.

"Why?"

"Because I became addicted to it. Addicted to the ritual, addicted
to the relief."

He considers her response while ashing his cigarette. "So you're angry at God, or you don't believe in Him?"

"Both." Amelia bites the inside of her cheek for comfort. "The god I was taught about was loving and forgiving and merciful. But the god I knew . . . the god I knew was so vicious and unjust that I decided, fuck that god. Fuck Him for Ebola, and stillbirth and rape and starvation, and Pedro sleeping in the hall, and me. That god is a torturer. I wouldn't worship that god." *SINNER! Kill the apostate!* ::THE SMELL OF HOLY WATER:: "But I mourned Him all the same."

Charlie shrugs. "I don't agree with you, but I can see from your point of view how it might look that way."

"It doesn't matter. I'm not trying to deconvert you or insult you."

"No way, I know. It's not important to me, I'm not a religious person. I believe in God and Jesus and stuff, but I don't go to church or anything. My parents raised me Catholic, so I guess I just believe what my parents taught me."

"You know, fasting is considered a sign of holiness in the Bible."

"Yeah? Well maybe I'll become a priest so I can starve myself in peace."

Amelia smears a smile across her face. "You could be a wrestling priest. There's a Christian wrestling center off the Brown line. You could work there and have the best of both worlds."

Charlie laughs. "That is not real." He is smiling now. He is losing his teeth but right now he is smiling.

"Is so. It's for at-risk youth. I read about it in *StreetWise*."

"Bullshit," he says, taking one last drag off his smoke. "Are you serious?"

"Dead serious."

"But not seriously dead," he says, reaching for the ashtray.

"Not yet," she concedes.

"Not yet."

Charlie puts out his cigarette.

THE REMOTE (PART II)

Amelia, Charlie, Maxwell, and Pedro sit at a table in the psych ward common room, playing cards. Her energy is frazzled as she says, "I would give anything to smoke a joint with you guys right now." In her mind, she sets out a bag that smells like the inside of a Fruity Pebbles box, and grinds up some choice bud. A cone would be better than a blunt, I think.

Pedro shakes his head. "That shit makes me paranoid. Wish I had some Xanax."

"Not me, I hate benzos," brags Maxwell. "They slow me down. I lose my edge." There are red 'hairs' on the soft, green mind-flowers. Red · · · Orange · · · Red · · · Big · · · And suddenly the Big Red gum jingle begins.

"I would DIE without Xanax," Charlie rolls his eyes dramatically. "It's the only thing that calms me down. But it gives me the munchies. I take one: fifteen minutes goes by and I'm stuffing my face—" Yes, yes, we all know that our fresh breath will go on and on "—then four hours after that I'm puking it all up." Amelia wonders if Charlie counts calories in gum, like she does. "But those four hours are so worth it."

Maxwell turns nasty. "You. Are. A. Faggot. Only girls do shit like that. Xanax is for pussies who can't deal with reality." He puts down his cards. "I'm fucking straightedge, man, no additives necessary—no drugs, no alcohol, no cigarettes. Just my mind." The jingle finally comes to an end.

"You were literally smoking a cigarette ten minutes ago in the lounge," says Charlie in exasperation.

"And you told me you were here for drugs," Amelia challenges.

He jumps up. "Fuck you, faggots, I'm going to watch *Judge Judy*."

"How are you doing, Pedro?" Amelia lays down a pair to the sound of another jingle: the 1989 Gillette razors riff. "Are they letting you sleep with the lights on?"

"No, I asked. I kind of freaked out over it and got taken down."

Looks go around the table ::SOUND OF A DIAL-UP MODEM CON-NECTING:: Charlie speaks first. "That sucks, dude."

"Yeah, well . . . I should've controlled myself." He lays out a hand. "It's just such an easy solution. I don't know why they won't just let me sleep with the lights on!"

"Maybe because you don't seem as sick, at first glance. One conversation with Maxwell, and you know he's crazy. One look at my arms, or at any of the freaks in here, and we're immediately recognized as mentally ill. But you and Charlie, and that guy Marvin," she gestures to Marvin, who is sitting on the couch reading a newspaper with his back to the television, "you seem like perfectly reasonable people. At least you have clothes." For fuck's sake · · · Now I gotta listen to Burger King commercials? Can I at least have something after 1995? she begs her brain.

"The hallucinations mostly happen in the dark. During the day I'm pretty normal. I mean, when I take my meds, but they pulled me off of everything to start over, and now . . ." His voice trails off.

"What kind of things do you see?" asks Charlie, impersonally ::THE HAMSTER DANCE SONG::

"It mostly has to do with things crawling into my ears and mouth and nose and eyes. I can feel the worms eating my brain . . . squirming. Parasites in my eyelashes, and bugs crawling all over, all over me."

"And green monsters, right?" asks Amelia. **Beedeebee bop bow dee-do do /**

"Well, that's the best way I could describe it at the time, but the monsters are really giant bacteria." The song continues on fast-forward.

"Oh, sorry," she says. Why don't you just kill yourself? That's never getting better. "How did you end up in here?

"I live with my parents, and they Baker Acted me. Seriously, it's a relief. At least I'll get some help."

THE CHANNEL SUDDENLY CHANGES

The room erupts into chaos. Orderlies frantically search for the remote and break up fights, while Amelia thinks that there is no good part of waking up, even with Folgers in your cup.

NONE TAKEN

A beautiful young Puerto Rican girl bursts through the door while Amelia is on the toilet. "Can you believe this bullshit?! That asshole puts me in here like some kinda joke? Fuck you, Tulio!" she yells to the ceiling, giving the bird with an over-manicured nail. "And fuck that skanky bitch you got on the side!"

Amelia pushes the toilet flush, and quietly rinses her hands without soap. She can smell that the girl is on her period. As if flowery perfume could cover the rusty stink of blood. The young woman talks at Amelia.

"I slashed this bitch's tires, spray-painted CHEATER on HIS car cuz he's a FUCKING cheater, and they call the cops and they put me in this place with you psychos. No offense."

Amelia goes very still. The scruff on her neck pricks up. "None taken." Offense has been taken.

"Isn't that just bullshit though? I am NOT a crazy person. This is BULLSHIT!" *Pull off the fingernails.*

"Yes. It is. Bullshit." *Crack the bones open and suck out the marrow.* "You don't belong here."

"For real!" Jasmine sizes up Amelia, and says, "You do that to yourself?"

"Yes."

"Somebody rape you or something?"

"No."

Jasmine sucks her teeth. "Well I don't know what your damage is, but you're obviously *psicópata*. I'm Jasmine."

"Amelia." *Shave the head. Burn it.* She does not move. The crow circles like a vulture.

"Well, Am-e-li-a, I'm here for three days, tops, so don't kill me in my sleep, okay?"

She plops down on the bed and starts braiding an inch-wide plait over her shoulder. Amelia is rooted to the spot. Every hair on her body is standing on end as she thinks about the girl's blood, bright on the colorless wall. Fascia pushes up and out of Jasmine's throat *tear it open with your teeth.* The light dimming in her eyes *GOUGE OUT THE EYES TAKE THE EYES OUT!* All of it is there in the infinite darkness of her brain. She's about my size; it would be a fair fight. *Bite her! Pluck it out!*

"I'm thinking about it," she tells her. "Hard."

THE BOTTOM

Amelia stares at the intimidating white trapezoid given to her by the medication nurse. *How the fuck am I going to swallow this? I can barely take Tylenol.* Rosemary starts complaining in line behind her, so she takes a mouthful of water, drops the pill in the very back of her throat, gags once, then manages to gulp it down. Amelia shows her tongue to the nurse before being dismissed to the common room.

Charlie must already be in bed, I don't see him. She starts a game of solitaire, but feels sleepy within minutes. Amelia stands to go to bed, and the room tilts. She has to sit back down to upright her torso. Her eyes go in and out of focus. Her breathing is heavy. *Where . . . where am I?* **Inhale exhale. Inhale exhale.** *Am I . . . What?* **Inhale exhale. Inhale exhale.** The walls and floor are warping under her feet. **Inhale exhale. Inhale exhale.** *This is . . . Is this Nine Inch Nails?* **Inhale exhale. Inhale exhale.** Trent Reznor's voice coaxes her toward the room.

Her eyes swim in their sockets. Everything is in slow motion. Leaning on furniture and the wall, Amelia plods toward her room. People are halos of darkness against the light. She does not know if they speak to her. The guitar keens. Trent whispers something she has never figured out as she falls face first onto her pathetic little bed and passes out cold. The tendrils of the song flick her ears as she sleeps long and hard.

Suddenly, he screams in her head, jerking her into confused consciousness. *What is that sound?* Her mind gropes the air to put a name on the vibrations. It's a scream. Someone's being tortured. It's a—

An orderly pokes her head in and says, "Fire drill. Get up and go stand by the exit."

The fire alarm is going off. Amelia's brain tunes it out in favor of "The Downward Spiral (The Bottom)." Her mind gropes for clarity. **Clicks and whispers.** She can barely stand. Instruments blip in and out · · · Wavering with her eyesight. 'The question is sleep.' Everything is still at half-speed. Am I awake? The drums signal that she is. 'The answer is Trazodone.' All the psych patients are being crowded into a narrow hallway, blocked by two thick, metal double doors that are locked. When Amelia sees it, the cellos groan. *EXIT.* She stares down the hallway as it distorts into an impossibly long white corridor.

Shoulda got a gun escape now Dasein cow stupid bitch my ears hurt. She drunkenly steadies herself against the wall, and makes her way to the area the geniuses who decided to have a fire drill at six a.m. in the psych ward have designated for this fire drill at six a.m. in the psych ward. The cellos moan again. I can't hear the alarm but my ears hurt. The disembodied hands type: *If any man come to me, and hate not his father and mother, and wife and children, and brethren and sisters, and his own life also, he cannot be my disciple.*

The emergency lights flash with the flutes. **Pulse—Pulse.** Clap your hands, Peter! She stops to watch them. **Pulse—Pulse.** Clap your hands! Tinkerbell is dying! People are pulling and pushing on their way, **Pulse—Pulse,** screaming in excitement and confusion and fear. **Pulse—Pulse.** She stands, fixated by the lights for an eight-measure eternity.

But because of your stubbornness and unrepentant heart, you are storing wrath against yourself for the Day of God's Wrath, when His righteous judgment will be revealed.

When Charlie finds Amelia plastered to the wall, staring at the flashing lights, **Pulse—Pulse,** he says something important, but Amelia can only hear a voice telling her how easy it is. Not real. Not his real voice · · · Not Charlie. Charlie speaks again, and Amelia shakes her head. **Baaaaaaaannnnnggg.** He leads her to the corridor, sits, and invites her into his lap. She buckles onto the hard floor. Robots are crawling through her brain cells, chewing on the synapses. Charlie pulls Amelia's head up onto his leg and tries to reassure her. **Baaaaaaaannnnnggg.** Mechanical spiders are replicating in her cells, replacing her human neurons. Her gaze is empty as she perceives the rest of her inmates going wild, while nurses try to control the crowd and take attendance. She squints. Maxwell is jauntily going from person to person to work them up. **Baaaaaaaannnnnggg.** Trent Reznor's distorted voice hits her mind like sound-braille. **Baaaaaaaannnnnggg.** Two people get taken down. So easy . . . Some are rocking and crying. Their ears hurt too flood in the ears infections of the brain. Lucia is screaming prayers, blood in the ears · · · Blood in the brain · · · The mute pees herself. When Maxwell punches the wall next to Rosemary's head, he gets taken down. **Baaaaaaaannnnnggg.** He does not go calmly. *Shoulda got a gun.* He kicks and screams and fights them, tooth and nail. **Baaaaaaaannnnnggg.** Amelia curls into a ball, unable to function. Charlie strokes her hair and tries to speak again. "**Baaaaaaaannnnnggg.**" All she can hear is the song. "They turned off the **Baaaaaaaannnnnggg.**" The man who swore to rape her hoots, "I can see her ass! Damn that's a cute ass. Can I get up in there?" Jack-off pulls down his boxers and takes his dick out, making straight for Amelia. **Baaaaaaaannnnnggg.** He is intercepted by Daniel. *Rape her · · · She WANTS it! Skullfuck her eye sockets and come in her brain and she'll THANK you for it!* He also fights them, tooth and nail.

Charlie's hand is still on her head. Her eyes gag on the room as everything starts to spin out of control.

I also gave them over to statutes that were not good, and laws they could not live by; I let them become defiled through their gifts · · · the sacrifice of every firstborn · · · that I might fill them with horror so they would know I am the Lord.

The nurses are trying to calm the remaining patients, now that the alarm has stopped. The limp guitar strums. The most dangerous patients have been subdued. Some are still crying and praying, and the piss runs down Juanita's leg into a pool at her feet. Amelia's mouth starts to water. "Daniel," she says. "Daniel, I'm gonna throw up." Somehow he hears her, or Charlie calls to him, she's not sure. They help Amelia to her bathroom. The Jack-in-the-box is clear in her mind. She is inside. It is bottomless.

All around the mulberry bush / The mon-key chased the wea-sel / La, la la, la lalala la / The vomit surges out of the bottomless pit. Her mouth pours saliva. **All around the mulberry bush / The mon-key chased the wea-sel / La, la, la, la lalala la /** Amelia vomits again. The clown mocks her · · · Bouncing on its spring. **All around the mulberry bush / The mon-key chased the wea-sel / La, la la, la lalala la /** More vomit comes gushing from Amelia's insides. **All around the mulberry bush / The mon-key chased the wea-sel / La, la, la, la lalala la /** Amelia vomits so hard that she can feel blood vessels exploding in her eyes. **Pop! goes the wea-sel.**

She collapses.

HOW DOES IT MAKE
YOU FEEL?

Amelia has been allowed to go back to sleep on a med pass, until lunch. Lying on her sticky plastic mattress, she studies her wounds as an audience applauds in her head for a long time. Something live, that's good. She anticipates the acoustic opening of "Nutshell" and is rewarded with Alice in Chains.

She slowly picks at the stitches in the crook of her left elbow. The skin on the top one pulls back as it loosens. She can see the white tissue underneath. The skin is red and raw as it starts to heal around the edges. *FLAY HER*, encourages a malicious voice. Amelia carefully takes the top stitch out, then starts to work on the second one. The voice massages her neck from behind, peering over her shoulder at her progress. After the second stitch is out, she is bleeding again. The voice clasps his wet, red hands in approval.

"Knock, knock!" Charlie appears in the doorway to Layne Staley's coos. "My aunt sent me these flowers, and I thought you need them more than I do. She even got a plastic vase, so I can keep them on the dresser. Er, you can keep them on . . ." He looks around the room, "You don't have a dresser." Amelia hides her arm from his view.

"Thank you, Charlie, but I need to rest." *Bleed the sick child. Get your leeches and maggots and ticks.*

"I just . . ." He lingers at the foot of her bed, flowers in hand. "I just wanted to hang out. Everyone else here is a lunatic."

"Charlie, I'M a lunatic," she retorts, irritably.

"Yeah, but you're interesting crazy, not syphilis crazy."

Everybody's clown. "Please don't use that word to describe me." The voice is displeased by the interruption. *Get rid of him!*

"We'll just chill then," he says, sitting on the edge of her bed. She can't look at him, but he smells like moors and cold wind and thistles. Full-scale cèilidh performance · · · Goddamnit, what the fuck is up with their weird little feet? "What did they give you?" he asks, oblivious to her mood.

"Trazodone."

"Just a sleeping pill? What's your dosage?"

"One hundred and fifty mg, and it's shaped like a fucking trapezoid. I can't believe I was actually able to choke it down." Amelia pictures a group of pharmaceutical reps trying to figure out how to *really sell* their product, Trazodone. I know! says one. TRAzodone · · · TRApezoid. We shape the pill into an inch-long trapezoid! The other reps pat him on the back and take an early lunch.

"Mo-ther-fuckers," he shakes his head.

"Best sleep I've ever had in my life," Amelia grudgingly admits.

He smiles, turns toward her, and puts his thigh on the bed. "Why do you hate it when people call you interesting? I mean, being interesting is a good thing. I've never met anyone like you before."

"Why? Because I'm not a fucking television set! My stories are not movies you can rewind just to see your favorite parts, and my misery is only poetry because I write it down as such."

"You shouldn't be offended," he counsels. "You can't not realize you bring it upon yourself. If you really hated it, you would pretend to be boring." *Sew the mouth SHUT!*

Amelia's eyes narrow. *Don't let her speak!* "I'm not going to dumb myself down to make people feel better about themselves." Pride, pride, pride, the archangel shakes his head.

"Then you're going to have to accept that you're interesting," he grins.

She bares her eyes. The song stops suddenly. The tension between them smells like the dentist.

Charlie's confidence gives a sharp pull to his esophagus. "I mean, you have so much to give but you're being torn apart—by fate, or illness, or God, whatever," he stammers. "That's not the point. The point is that you live honestly, and that's why I care about you." Amelia's affect turns completely neutral. *You have no fucking clue how I live. None of you do.* Instead of Charlie, she thinks about her successful failure of a life and the inertia cause by freedom of choice. Original sin. The angels scream, *FILTHY! FILTHY! FILTHY!* in her head. *You bring it upon yourself.* "And you're important to me. I mean, it would be cool if we could see each other when we get out. It would be nice to have someone to talk to about life on the inside." Amelia doesn't respond. A romantic vision of a suicide pact between her and Charlie presents itself to her. "I think you're beautiful and unique, and I want you around," he tries. *Bite the wine glass. Slash the mouth to bits. Crunching between the teeth · · · Shards in the gums.* Charlie stands up. "Well, say something. I mean, how does that make you feel?"

The last chorus of "How Does It Make You Feel?" by Air bursts into Amelia's head. She considers his words through a screen of music. How does it make me feel? *You bring it on yourself.* How does it make me feel? *If you really hated it, you would pretend.* How does it make me feel? Charlie can see the sudden change in her, not knowing that it is music freezing her expression and not him. How does it make me feel? He waits and holds her gaze.

When Amelia finally speaks, all she can say is, "'Well, I really think you should quit smoking.'"

AWAKE SOON

Daniel passes Amelia in the hallway. "You're bleeding."

Amelia angles her arm away from Daniel's sight. "Yeah, some of my stitches came out."

"Came out? Let me see." He takes her arm and looks at the opening wound. "Goddamnit, Amelia! Really? You're going to need this stitched up like now."

"It's okay," she shrugs out of his grip.

"It's not okay. You can't mutilate yourself here, no matter what your tactics are," he excoriates her. "Go to your room and wait for Nurse Rhonda. I'm not wasting my time with this shit. You know better."

"Fine!" Amelia storms back to her room, gets on the bed, and waits. She lies on her back, staring at the ceiling, and requests a song. *Awake Soon, by Sara,* the disembodied hands type. Sarah with an H, Amelia reminds them. *Sara-h Slean.* On command, the song appears. Sarah's voice is clear and clean in timbre. A singer harmonizing perfectly with herself · · · The brilliant lyrics . . . The *Blue Parade* album always comforted her in dark times. The singer's voice peals like the church bells ringing as she played on the railroad tracks in Rincon, Georgia, as a child. No vibrato.

Nurse Rhonda appears. An endless fermata sustains the chord in her mind. The nurse drags a chair into Amelia's room, screeching the feet against the floor. She kicks it close to Amelia's bed and tosses her bag on it, then glares.

"It is my understanding that you have removed several of your stitches. You should know that I find it quite irritating that I have to take time off my work to sew new ones," she admonishes Amelia, who is up for the challenge.

"Isn't this part of your job? Not my fault you don't have good time-management skills," she replies, sitting up.

"No, lay where you are," says the nurse, prepping her sterile instruments and thread. "You're right: I don't have time. In fact, I didn't even have enough time to get the local anesthetic." She bares her teeth at Amelia. "But you're tough enough to pull out stitches, I'm sure you're tough enough to do this without analgesic."

Amelia's eyes are ablaze. "I don't need it."

"Good," says the nurse, "because I'm not spending a single second looking for it."

Nurse Rhonda places the first stitch. "Awake Soon" resumes while she repairs Amelia's arm. Hanging by the teeth on the edge of a plain wooden table suspended over a desert canyon. Splintering · · · Frothy, foamy, loose around the gums. The stitches don't hurt. Chris begging to have her back. Sarah inhales her own breath like warm steam · · · Not a single cent off.

The nurse seems unsatisfied by Amelia's calm demeanor, so she picks at her. "I don't understand why you people do this. You know, if you just prayed, God would heal you." *IT'S A TRAP!*

"Every suicide ever is god's fault: he gives People more than They can bear."

The woman gives Amelia an ugly polystyrene smile. "He could fill you with the Joy of the Spirit, you need only repent." Amelia knows what repentance is. Repentance is showing God that you're willing to pay for your own sins; that you don't want to make His son a scapegoat. "Tell God that you are wicked and unworthy, and He will make you happy again."

Amelia can't help but let her anger rise. "I have repented. Fifty-two times. And I have the scars to prove it. I trusted God. I leaned on Him, I knelt at His feet, I plead with Him, I BEGGED Him. I lived according to His word and love. I watched others be healed while I fell at His feet, and you know what happened?" Nurse Rhonda looks unimpressed. "NOTHING." The woman pulls the thread sharply. "If I cannot be healed by that amount of faith, I cannot be healed."

"That's not true," the nurse ties off the last stitch. "God always answers the prayers of the faithful. But sometimes the answer is 'No.'" She snips the thread with blunted scissors.

The song abandons Amelia on the last note, and her fangs pulse with venom. "FUCK YOU, you fucking bitch! How dare you? How dare you imply that I choose to feel this way, that I somehow DESERVE the desire to slice off my feet and cut my eyes out of my face!" Nurse Rhonda gathers her equipment and starts for the door. "Yes, please, get the fuck out of here and don't ever come near me again."

On her way out, the nurse picks up the small trashcan in the bathroom, snatches Charlie's flowers off the shelf, and throws them in, vase and all. CUNT! The nurse smiles smugly. "I thought I'd made it clear that you are not to have potentially dangerous items, especially now that you have caused yourself injury. Think about that."

Amelia is left seething.

CHOCOLATE JESUS

The group prays as a washtub bass plucks in Amelia's mind. Tom Waits's voice scratches the ceiling of her inner ear, and she can't help but smirk in the roof of her mouth as he praises his "Chocolate Jesus." It fades when Nurse Jessica begins talking.

"Amen. Today, we're talking about building relationships—healthy relationships." Chris. *SELFISH BITCH!* "What does it mean to have a healthy relationship?"

The song cuts off entirely when Amelia's roommate starts talking with her fingernails. "It's not fucking assholes like Tulio; cheating lying son-of-a-bitches who screw any skank that walks by! I got back at him, and they put me in here!"

Charlie is game. "What did you do?"

"I keyed his car and bashed in the headlights and slashed her fuckin' tires! And I spray-painted 'CHEATER' across his windshield cuz he DESERVES it!"

"And what do YOU deserve?" Nurse Jessica asks. There is a pause. "What are some qualities in a partner you think could be healthy, Jasmine?"

"Well," the girl says, "just, like, not being a dick all the time and lying and cheating."

"So," the nurse rephrases for her, "honesty, loyalty, and a sense of companionship. Try saying that out loud: 'I deserve honesty, loyalty, and a sense of companionship.' Everyone pair up and try it. I will be John's partner."

Charlie and Amelia pair up as Nurse Jessica sits with the

comatose man. Amelia whispers it under her breath: "I deserve honesty, loyalty, and a sense of companionship." This is so fucking stupid. But when Charlie says it, they find genuine connection in the moment. He thinks I am valuable. Look at the little spots in his eyeballs from purging. Yes. Beautiful.

Rosemary's voice rises above the murmur. "I want what? Are you asking me for sex, young man? Well I don't fuck brown people!" Pedro holds his hands up in the air. "I could fire you! I could fire you right now!" threatens Rosemary.

"FIRE HIM!" shouts Maxwell.

Nurse Jessica snaps her fingers. "Okay, back in the circle. Take a deep breath. Hands to yourself, Maxwell. Thank you. Can anyone tell me what we were just talking about?"

"Healthy relationships," says Marvin.

"Good listening! Thank you, Marvin," beams the nurse. "Healthy relationships. Marvin, what are some qualities you look for in a partner?"

"Oh, my wife is a saint. She deals with my late hours at work, the kids, and my imbalances. She's an angel. You'd like her."

"So: patience, strength, and stability. Very nice." Tom Waits goes on about unacceptable substitutes for Christ. "Charlie, what about you? What are you looking for in a partner?" Amelia becomes interested, and the song fades but does not pause.

Charlie looks embarrassed. "It's hard to say . . . I've never had a girlfriend."

Maxwell explodes with laughter, pointing at Charlie. "You ARE a faggot! Goddamnit, I thought it was the Mexican! It's you!" He collapses in fits of loud cackles.

Amelia jumps to Charlie's defense. "Fuck you, you psycho! You can't tell me you haven't sucked dick for drugs before!"

Maxwell stops laughing, and his third eyelid flashes, menacingly. "You're calling ME a psycho? At least I don't MURDER myself, you fucking freak."

"It sounds like both of you," interrupts the nurse, "need partners who are stable, supportive, and patient. Is that about right?" After a tense moment, they nod to the nurse and sit back down. She resumes the session. "Charlie, you were saying?" Harmonica solo.

"I've never had a girlfriend." Charlie wipes his palms on his CK flannel pants. "He's not the only one who thinks I'm gay—my father is terrified of it. It just was never important to me. It's not like I'm a virgin. If I want to get laid, I know where to find women. But . . . I want one as skinny as I am, who understands my eating disorder and maybe has one of her own. And we're sick in the head together, but we're also competing on the scale for fun, too. I know it sounds shallow, but I can only be with a woman who weighs less than my dog."

Jasmine's eyes go wide. "That's fucked up," she says.

He shifts uncomfortably. "He's a big dog." Charlie keeps his eyes on the floor.

"See? He IS gay!" yelps Maxwell. "He only likes girls that look like boys. NO titties on them chicks, man!"

Nurse Jessica returns to the topic while Waits gives advice on what to do with your savior, should He be melting on a hot day. "And what about some non-physical qualities?"

"Oh, um, I guess someone . . ." His eyes flick around the room. "Well, wild . . . and original, and . . . smart."

"So: free-spirited, unique, and intelligent." Amelia agrees that Jesus would make an excellent parfait. "I think you will be successful when you start seeing women for who they are, not what they weigh." The nurse turns to the ancient woman. "Rosemary? Why did you marry your husband?"

"Because he was rich," she says. "He wasn't particularly nice, but he took me to the classiest places, the classiest people, the jazz, the LIQUOR!" Rosemary becomes more animated. "I got to live exactly the life I wanted to have, and all I had to do was fuck him! Best decision I ever made."

"So," the nurse opens her mouth to summarize, "financial security, social availabi—"

"No, you little idiot, MONEY! All you need in this life is money!" Rosemary points to Jasmine. "You. Spic slut. Marry up."

"Fuck you, abuela," Jasmine says with her middle finger up. "I'm not even gonna respond with that." The harmonica whines again.

"Eyes to me," calls the nurse. "Thank you. Pedro? What qualities do you look for in a partner?"

"Um . . . balance. And kindness and religiousness."

"Very good," she approves. "Amelia?"

I'm not playing this stupid game. "My fiance just left me after being together for eight years. I hope no one ever touches me again."

"What about down the road, when you're ready to have a relationship?" the nurse pushes.

"I'm planning to be dead before that happens."

"So," Nurse Jessica says what she has been waiting to say the entire session, "redemption. A relationship with Christ."

"There's no redemption for me," Amelia cuts her eyes at the nurse. "I deny the Holy Spirit."

STABAT MATER

Amelia creates a Stabat Mater in her head as she sits with her father in the grubby common room.

Pro peccatis suae gentis vidit Iesum in tormentis et flagellis subditum /

"Daddy?" she breaks the silence. "Do you think I'm cursed? Like maybe I did something horrible in a past life, and am paying for it now?"

"No Amelia you are not cursed. You are loved. By me and the family and your friends." Her father looks pained. "Noah and Constance are coming next week."

"I don't want them to see me like this," she resists.

Vidit cuum dulcem natum moriendo desolatum dum emisit spiritum /

"They want to come support you," he says.

"I need to be left alone. I'll settle this." Amelia cannot deal with more humiliation within these walls.

"You NEED help," he says sharply. "It is being given to you. Accept it."

"It's just the worst kind of attent—"

"It is, but that's how things are, so you're going to have to deal with it. What did you expect? That we'd just ignore it?"

"You've been ignoring it for the past ten years."

Eia Mater, fons amoris, me sentire vim doloris fac ut tecum lugeam /

"I'm sorry . . . I didn't mean that."

"No, you're right. We have." Amelia's father takes off his glasses and rubs his bright blue eyes. "We did. I . . . I've been afraid of it since you were a child, having violent nightmares at three years old. The high IQ, the INTENSITY. You were always so INTENSE. So smart and so funny and so wonderful, but INTENSE. And dark. I don't know where you got that from."

Sancta Mater, istud agas, crucifixi fige plagas cordi meo valide /

"And I took you to church and gave you to those vultures." He opens his hands apologetically. "I thought they could help you, and those Christian counselors you saw in high school—we thought they'd help you. I was too ignorant to know that you were sick. You just seemed brilliant to everyone. And intense. All these mistakes we made, all these red flags we ignored . . . I just didn't know what to do."

Tui nati vulnerati tam dignati pro me pati poenas mecum divide /

She has to ameliorate his regret. "It's okay."

Mecum divide /

"We actually made decisions that were WORSE for you, and I'm so sorry. Those church people . . . you're not bad or evil . . . there's just something not quite right with your brain."

"You don't think I'm a bad person?"

Pro me pati poenas mecum divide /

I may share the pain /

"That God just hates me?"

Fac me vere tecum flere crucifixo condolere donec ego vixero /

"No, you're not a bad person. And God . . ." He briefly steeples his fingers on either side of his nose. "Well, all this has made me think about that very hard. I can't see any purpose in your suffering. I've seen a lot of suffering in my line of work, and I MUST believe that, ultimately, good people are rewarded and bad people are punished."

"But I'm being punished even though I did nothing wrong."

Iuxta crucem tecum stare te libenter sociare in planctu desidero /

Amelia's father shakes his head apologetically. "I don't understand it. My god wouldn't do that. Not a loving god. Not a FAIR god."

"Maybe He does it for fun. Like Job . . . Or at least allows it through indifference."

"Well things are not that black and white, Amelia. There is a whole spectrum between the two that you cannot see—"

"I think an indifferent god is worse than a malevolent one."

Mihi iam non sis amara fac me tecum plangere /
Be not bitter with me, let me weep with thee /

Amelia's father looks at her with defeat in his eyes. "I don't know if you're right."

Mihi iam non sis amara fac me tecum plangere /
Be not bitter with me, let me weep with thee

WALK THE LINE

After dinner, Amelia plays solitaire while the others smoke. Two orderlies wheel in a skeletal young woman while Amelia listens to Johnny Cash and the kindergarteners play hopscotch. The woman looks frail, with thinning blonde hair and a pinched, unattractive face. Amelia is surprised by her odd, high-pitched voice.

"Que pasa, Pedro?"

"Nada," he smiles. "You got back fast."

The woman turns to Amelia and squeaks, "You're new. I'm Susanna. Today is my thirty-second birthday and I'm very upset that I'm not dead."

"That makes two of us." Obviously anorexia and depression, but she smells like something else, too. "I'm Amelia." They nod to each other. I can't put my finger on it . . . The kindergarteners disappear as Johnny grumbles, then Charlie walks into the room and sees Susanna.

"Hey, hey! You're back already?"

She gives him a clumsy wave. "Yeah, well, I thought I'd try to kill myself again, but I wanted to do something new so I thought, 'What about playing in traffic?'"

"Cheeky," Amelia says, impressed by the choice. Charlie looks her over.

"How'd it work out?"

"I'm alive, so, terrible," Susanna complains. "I'm such a failure I can't even kill myself right. How pathetic is that? I've tried slitting my wrists, jumping from a bridge, starving myself to death, overdose, poison, hanging—something always goes wrong!"

Amelia's mouth hints at a smile. Susanna talks like Shirley Henderson.

"This was my seventh try, and I wanted it to be special cuz lucky number seven, right? So I took the bus to Cicero and drove my chair into the oncoming cars, and they all swerved and honked and not a SINGLE ONE hit me!"

Charlie cracks up at the scowl on her face.

"So, the cops start chasing me, but my chair goes up to just like a LITTLE faster than they could run. I was pissed because I knew I wasn't gonna die, so I just let them chase me all over the highway until my battery ran down."

Charlie and Pedro are laughing while Amelia imagines the scene over the *Benny Hill* theme.

"Not only did they throw me back in here, but they're also gonna charge me with evading arrest! It's bullshit!"

Susanna's attendant reappears with a tray of food for her.

"What the fuck is this?" She examines her food in disgust. A cow patty covered in old bovine breast milk between two slabs of particleboard. "This is a cheeseburger. A cheeseburger. What the fuck am I supposed to do with a cheeseburger?"

If Amelia were able to feel anything related to pleasure, she might laugh.

"I fucking hate food," continues Susanna. "I choke down two hundred calories a day, and instead of bringing me something I might eat, like a salad or some fruit, you bring me a fucking cheese-burger?" She pushes the plate off of her wheelchair tray with her good hand.

Damn, thinks Amelia, that's commitment.

SOMETHING I CAN
NEVER HAVE

The art room is buzzing with talk as people color in paper mandalas. Amelia is sitting next to Charlie, drawing a tiny robot in every blank space on the mandala with a golf pencil, hearing the mechanical, whipping noise of Nine Inch Nails's "Something I Can Never Have" over and over again.

Charlie peers at her paper. "Why do you do robots?"

"I'm afraid of robots," she answers.

"So why put them on everything?"

"I understand robots," Amelia elaborates. "I know what it's like to be able to think but not feel." She sketches out another robot in the neighboring space.

"How can you not feel, but want to die? Don't you have to be sad to want to die?"

"It's worse than pain. Much worse than sadness. *Anhedonia*. That's what they call it in the psych world. The inability to feel pleasure." She thinks of the increasingly extreme lengths she has to go to in order to achieve orgasm.

"Well, that's got to be better than wanting to kill yourself," says Charlie.

"The two are not mutually exclusive," she corrects him. "They happen at the same time. Since I don't feel anything, I am overcome by my thoughts. And my thoughts say, 'Kill! Kill! Kill! Kill!'" *KILL! KILL! KILL!* "There is nothing inherently redeeming about life."

Charlie looks at her with wide eyes. "Doesn't that bother you?"

"Which part?" Pincer claws or spider hands?

"That there's a voice in your head telling you to kill yourself."

"Multiple voices. It's like a fucking cheerleading squad." Amelia decides on spider hands. "Of course it bothers me. And I would do anything to escape it. ANYTHING." They both glance down at her bandages. "Wouldn't you?" Charlie doesn't respond. "What kind of a life is that, anyway? What purpose could my suffering possibly serve?"

"You don't think life has meaning?"

"Life is a cruel joke." She moves one space over and begins another robot. "Great childhood, no history of abuse, nothing bad has ever happened to me. I've never even had someone close to me die. All four grandparents alive and healthy, parents happily married for thirty years. I did have love and family and friends, but no ability to enjoy it." *You're an ungrateful bitch. I hope you DO kill yourself and go straight to Hell where you belong.* "I'm just made wrong. What I've endured in my head doesn't match my life. I should be a refugee in a third-world country, who has lost husbands and children. I should be raped and have my breasts cut off and be left for dead." At least, then, I'd be dead. "But I'm not. I'm a middle-class white girl in America at the turn of the millennium. It's so wrong."

"Yeah, my parents don't understand it at all. I'm a poor little rich boy," he says. "They think I'm obsessed with being thin, but I'm really obsessed with being LIGHT."

"I've never met a guy with an eating disorder," says Amelia.

"Yes you have, you just didn't know about it," he replies.

Amelia thinks about Olympic wrestlers weighing in before a match, cheering at the numbers on the scale. "So it's not just a girl thing?"

"Oh my God, please don't say that. That is so fucking offensive. That's like me calling you interesting."

"Sorry." Another robot crawls from her fingers onto the paper.

"It's okay, it's just, that's what everyone thinks. It's definitely what my dad thinks. They don't understand that the more you try to control food, the more it controls you."

Amelia considers the notebook she burned along with her journals before her suicide: ninety pages of clippings from magazines of impossibly thin women to give her 'thinspiration' to distract her when she felt hungry. "Plus, it's not just women who are told what they should look like in the media. Guys have that pressure, too."

He shakes his head. "Honestly, it doesn't have shit to do with the media. I've been heavy and I've been light, and I prefer being light. I like myself better this way."

"But you hate the disorder," she reminds him.

"Yes." Charlie chooses a bright orange colored pencil for his mandala. "Why do you do it? Other than trying to starve yourself to death. It's got to be more complicated than that."

Amelia sketches a large robot looming over the mandala, claws poised to snatch a smaller robot off the page. "For me, it's just the only part of myself that I can control. It's slow pain. For instance: I was on my way to Dominick's awhile back, worrying about lunch. I didn't have anything for breakfast, so I was feeling really good like I could only eat three strawberries for lunch, which is a weird goal I've had for a really long time; I don't know why. But then I was thinking I should eat more so I don't binge at night. But then I saw the lunch special which was a yummy turkey wrap and I wanted it SO badly, but THEN, oh yes, THEN I saw that they had a tray of little slices for tasting. So I took a slice, and got a tiny bit of trail mix and two pieces of pineapple because there weren't any strawberries. And I didn't burn myself that day."

The fat therapist interrupts them. "Amelia? What is with these robots?"

"I don't know. I just like them," she says.

"Well, it's making our interpretation sessions very boring. Let's try to follow directions next time. Yes?"

Amelia nods and puts the stubby pencil back in its plastic cup.

THE WAY I AM

Amelia is sitting alone in the common room listening to Eminem while her friends smoke in the lounge. Her blood runs with the beat as Nurse Rhonda makes her way to each person, taking vitals and distributing medication. Amelia stares daggers at her. After the left half of the room has their pills, she starts toward Amelia with her blood pressure cuff and tray of pills and water.

Amelia jumps up as the woman approaches. "I don't know what you think you're doing. Coming up to me like you're gonna TOUCH me, you stupid cowbitch piece of shit." She slaps away the blood pressure cuff, upsets the pill cup Nurse Rhonda is holding, and throws the water in her face. "Get the fuck away from me! Moooo! You fucking BITCH. You stupid fucking COW!"

Daniel appears while the nurse sputters. "Whoa, whoa. What's going on here?"

"This stupid bitch—" Amelia points at Nurse Rhonda.

"An incident of assault needs to be filed on this woman," interrupts the nurse.

"Assault?" Amelia paces to the beat of the song. "Are you fucking serious? Daniel, I told this cow not to come near me. She stitched me up WITHOUT ANESTHETIC, Daniel! She threw away my flowers!"

To Amelia, he says, "YOU may not make any aggressive gestures toward staff," then turns to Rhonda. "And YOU know better. Walk away."

"I'm charting this as assault," says the nurse as she grabs the monitor off the floor. "And I'm not picking that up." The pill has skittered across the room.

"I've got it," Daniel says, stooping down as the nurse walks away. "Just Trazodone, right?"

"Yes. One inch-long trapezoid."

Amelia's esophagus contracts at the sight of the powdery, sharp mind-candy.

"You feeling alright?" he checks.

"Yeah, it was just that first day I felt like shit. Sleeping like a baby now."

Daniel hands the pill to Amelia. "Take this. Go to sleep. And don't ever threaten that lady again."

TESTIFY

It's time for group therapy and Amelia is so keyed up that her jaw hurts from grinding her teeth.

"Let us pray," says Nurse Jessica. Everyone except Amelia joins hands. A guitar rides the key of **D**, hard and distorted. Brad Wilk is the consummate drummer. De la rocha calls to her through the microphone. The prayer is over in measures. Amelia's body is tense and unstable as a Tesla coil.

"Amen." She starts the session. "Jasmine? I know you had an important phone call today. Is there anything you'd like to discuss?"

Jasmine is less attractive by half without makeup, but still talks like an 8. "Well, um, you're all a bunch of psychos, and I'm not sharing any secrets with you." Nurse Jessica looks at her disapprovingly.

"I accept your decision not to share, but please do not use words like 'psycho,' or 'crazy,' or 'mental.' We're all human beings here, and deserve to be treated with respect."

"Yeah, well," Jasmine sucks her teeth, "Imma just do me til I get out tomorrow."

"Nurse Jessica?" Pedro raises his hand. "Can we maybe talk about some good ways to tell if something is real or not?"

He has an air of desperation in his voice, but Amelia only hears the song, compelled by it to attack any weakness in sight.

"What an excellent conversation topic!" the nurse praises him. "Please start whenever you're ready."

"Okay. Um, well, I heard Amelia say that she thinks there might be bugs in the food, and now I can't stop seeing hairy little legs and wings in everything, and it's making things really hard for me."

"Well, perhaps Amelia would like to address this herself?" Nurse Jessica gives her the chance to explain.

The music affects the rhythm of Amelia's speech. "Yeah, here's the thing, there are all KINDS of bug parts and rat feces in our food, so I don't know what you want me to do about it. I spit it out, too."

"But you're not schizophrenic!"

"I don't think there's anything crazy about being sickened by insect parts and rat shit." The guitar comes in heavy and rough.

"Okay, can you just tell me how to tell the difference?" he pleads with Nurse Jessica.

"Who has ideas on how to reality-check yourself?" asks the nurse.

The music builds to a frantic, driving force that propels Amelia's aggression forward. She descends on Pedro. "It's YOUR reality. YOUR reality includes bugs in your food, and bacteria, and parasites, that's YOUR reality! You're stuck! God fucked you over and you're STUCK here with it! Suffer through it or kill yourself, man, because that is the REST OF YOUR LIFE."

"I think that is VERY bad advice," Nurse Jessica takes over. "I will personally come up with a plan of action for your episodes."

Rage Against the Machine blasts holes between Amelia's ears · · · Holes that fill with blood and fluid to grow songs in the soft womb of destroyed brain matter.

"Let's leave this conversation for later, and move on to the main focus of today's session: making goals for the future. We each get a marker and a piece of paper." The nurse hands out the materials. "You're going to mark your paper one to three in bullets, and then write three goals for yourself. They don't have to be big things; small steps are important, too. Small steps lead to large steps."

Amelia gets a black marker and huffs a tiny laugh at her idea, then immerses herself in the song.

"Think about your goals . . . even something like brushing your teeth every day can be a good goal."

The patients write and Nurse Jessica does one for herself.

"Okay, let's share. My goals are: be a better listener, exercise more, and eat more vegetables. Pedro?"

"Take my meds every day, do the relaxation breathing thing, and lose weight," he says.

"Very good. Let's keep going around the circle," says the nurse.

The guitar solo urges Amelia to finish the bullets before her turn.

Susanna holds her paper in an obscenely fleshless hand. "Eat less, weigh less, sleep more." She used a pink marker.

"Jasmine?"

"No more of these fucking *guillaos*, no more *perico*, get my GED," the girl participates.

"Spend more time with my son," smiles Marvin. "Show more affection to my wife, and get my Mastercard paid off."

Maxwell makes a rude gesture: "Fuck more, have more sex, and make more looooove."

"Charlie?" asks the nurse.

"Um, get back into school and stop purging . . ." Amelia isn't listening to him. "Maybe . . . quit smoking?"

Nurse Jessica nods. "An excellent goal. Amelia?"

Amelia turns her paper around so that the nurse can see it.

It's a gun blowing off a stick figure's head, with three bullets. Amelia smiles sarcastically.

"That's enough out of you, Amelia," clips the nurse. "You're dismissed."

Amelia climbs on the song and speeds out of the room on its current.

R.E.M.

At the nurse's station, Daniel is going through a bag while Amelia and her father watch. Her tendons twitch with the piano movements of the most normal song she can think of, struggling to regain her composure after Group. I can't believe you took your fucking stitches out.

Daniel pulls the straps on the bag, and begins explaining what she can and cannot have. "Obviously, we can't give her the actual bag, because of the straps. No to the pants, could hang herself with the leg material there. No to the bra, hanging again, no to the sweatshirt, same." Come on, at least let me wear a bra! "I'm sorry but we can't give her any of this liquid stuff: shampoo, conditioner, contact solution, toothpaste . . . poison, you see." The song changes, adding strings. "No to the underwear, hanging again. You'd be surprised by how many simple objects can be dangerous." FUCKER! "Definitely no to the hairbrush. She could use that as a weapon. I'm afraid I can't give her anything in here, Mr. Adams."

Amelia's clown face cracks for an instant. "This is bullshit, Daniel!" Calm down. Be normal. Be normal. Be normal.

Her father steps in. "She needs contact solution. It's not healthy to sleep in dirty contacts."

The piano repeats its constant, comforting pattern, and lulls her back into her circus act.

"I'm sorry, but it's a risk analysis on our part," explains Daniel. "Every one of these items is no longer permitted because someone has successfully used them to self-harm. We've overlooked nothing.

If you go into the rooms, you can see that there are no electrical cords, no curtains, no loose parts; the bed is only four inches off the floor, blankets are short or sewn to the mattress, nothing protrudes from the wall, including water faucets."

This song is BORing! complains a kindergartener. "Nightswimming" is a classic, Amelia responds.

"The showers are kept at a safe temperature that cannot be changed by patients or staff, and all edged surfaces round down, so she can't injure herself or use them as a platform for hanging. So, believe me when I say: your daughter is safe, and can use her own things when she is discharged."

The piano continues its bouncy chords as Amelia's father nods sadly and bids her goodbye.

She leans over the counter.

"Fuck you, Daniel."

He is unapologetic. "You're the one who took your stitches out."

PINK ROBOTS

A tall woman with functional glasses checks in at the visitors' log. An acoustic guitar strums four bars of Constance's theme music in Amelia's mind, then drums kick when the door opens. "Yoshimi Battles the Pink Robots: Part 1" by The Flaming Lips has long been the musical equivalent of their friendship. Once Constance steps into the room, she goes toward Amelia as if to give her a hug.

Amelia holds up her arms to stop her from coming closer. "Don't, you can't. You're not allowed to touch me." The song resigns to the background.

"Jesus, Amelia, that looks terrible!" She wrings her long, thin fingers. "Does it hurt?"

"It mostly itches," she says, honestly.

"That means it's starting to heal." Constance adjusts her glasses and peers at the flesh above the bandage line. "Couldn't they do anything for your . . . elbows?" She gestures to her own inner elbows. "Are these elbows?"

"I think it's called a 'crook.' Gross, I know, but the bandages don't stay on so . . ."

"I'd hate to see what the rest look like," she says.

Amelia turns her elbows slightly outward so that the stitches are hidden from the front. "Yeah, I'm not looking forward to wearing long sleeves for the rest of my life." Hoping to change the subject, she pulls a plastic chair from under the nearest table. "Let's sit down over here."

Constance sits, and can't help but glance around the common room to gauge its expense.

"How long do you have to wear the bandages?"

"Until the stitches are ready to come out. Should be another two weeks or so."

"That sucks." Constance taps her fingers together awkwardly.

"Yeah, but most of the stitches are pretty tidy, so the outside scars shouldn't be too bad. It's the internal scarring I'm worried about. I missed most of the tendons, but severed some nerves."

"Oh my God!" exclaims the girl who requests her packaged Ramen noodles al dente. "Can you still play?"

Amelia methodically tests each finger. The tip of her right middle finger is numb, but functional. "Yes. At least, the doctor said I would, though I might have some issues with pressure. That doesn't really matter because the action of my piano is so immediate that pressure won't be an issue."

"Well that's good." The young woman's shoulders hunch in relief. "The house wouldn't be the same without music."

"I wouldn't be the same without music."

"Last Sunday dinner, right before I left for Florida, I thought I'd DIE laughing—" Her big green eyes go wide with regret at this word choice. "—at that stupid song you played on the autoharp about the dog." The stupid autoharp dog song starts playing in Amelia's head. She pretends to smile. Constance screws up her mouth. "Can I still say things like that? Like I thought I'd die or kill myself and stuff?"

"Yeah, I don't care."

"Are you sure?" she asks, trying to make up for her faux pas. "It seems so insensitive now."

"It's only insensitive if it's directed at me," Amelia says without expression.

Constance relaxes and brushes her bangs away from her glasses. "Okay, good, because I don't know if I could give it up."

"I would never ask such a thing," Amelia reassures her. "I'M the one who can't joke about it anymore."

"True."

They share a heavy look. Amelia looks down at the table and whispers, "Have you talked to Chris?"

"Yes," she answers cautiously. "He's—" Tact evades her. "—furious. Actually . . . everybody is. I've been tasked to tell you that they feel betrayed."

GUILTY!

Shame drops onto Amelia from above like an ACME anvil. "That's not—"

SELFISH!

Constance stops her. "I know! I'm the one who's been telling them: this isn't about you, this is about HER and her DEMONS. And if you think she has no demons, then you don't know her at all."

"Thank you." Amelia is grateful that at least one person can see it from her perspective. "You're a good friend." *I hope you DO die and go straight to Hell where you belong.* "The only thing worse than still being alive is having everyone angry at me. Did nobody get my letters?"

"Everybody got them. That's part of the reason they're mad."

"That doesn't make any sense." *I spent weeks on those letters.*

"Well, yeah, it sort of does. That's how they knew it wasn't just a cry for help . . ." She struggles for the right words and fails. "It was creepy."

"Creepy." Amelia's heart gives two hard beats, and anger flashes behind her eyes.

"Yeah," says Constance, sheepishly.

Lucia wanders into their vicinity, her Spanish praying getting louder and louder.

Amelia bristles. "Sorry, I didn't mean to be a weirdo. I thought everyone would appreciate a personal goodbye."

"No one 'appreciates' suicide notes, Amelia."

Lucia is suddenly at their table, shouting at Amelia in Spanish. Prokofiev crashes into her head. "The Fight." The horns come in from above, drilling into Amelia's mind with the woman's words. *"Dios te salve María: llenaeres de GRACIA, el Señor ES CONTIGO!"*

Amelia stands up, crackling with aggression. "Stay the fuck away from me! I don't want anything to do with your god!"

"Bendita tú eres entre todas las mujeres y bendito es el fruto de tu vientre!" Lucia walks in circles around Amelia, chanting her prayers. Constance backs away as Daniel jogs over from across the room.

The crow is poised on the edge of attack. Talons sharp. Eyes clear.

"YOUR. FAITH. MEANS. NOTHING!" yells Amelia.

I DENY THE HOLY SPIRIT!

"Jesús!" she wails. *"SANTA MARIA! Madre de Dios ruega por—"*

KILL THE APOSTATE!

"I can't understand what you're saying. Speak fucking English! *TU DIO ES NADA!"*

"—nosotros pecadores ahora y en la hora —"

Amelia's brain screams with trombones and caws of the murder.

"SPEAK ENGLISH!"

"—de nuestra MUERTE!"

Daniel breaks it up. "Ladies, what's going on? *Que pasa?"* Lucia is shouting amen repeatedly.

Amelia's body is tense as a violin bow. "Does she ever shut up?"

"Not that I've seen," he says, positioning his body between the two. He makes a placating gesture to Amelia. "You know what she's like. Stop letting her provoke you." Daniel faces Lucia and speaks quietly to her. *"Calmate. Calmate. Con su pan se lo coma. El sol brilla para todos. Calmate y hacer una siesta."* He leads the woman away as she mumbles and casts the evil eye at Amelia.

Constance is still standing in place, her face frozen in shock, as the brass re-enters. Shit. "I'm actually gonna head out."

Amelia's anger drops to zero and she puts her clown face back on. "I'm good. It's cool. Just . . . crazy people, man." She doesn't make eye contact.

"No, I've got this thing for class," says her friend. "But I'll come back."

Amelia meets her gaze.

"I'll come back."

THE DIAGNOSIS

Amelia waits in the doctor's office, sitting in a small chair across from a large desk. Pergolesi pulses in her head: minor, then dissonant, then minor, then root. *Take out the eyes. Sew the mouth shut. Kill it in the womb. Bury it in the ground.* The suspension. Violins repeat as she stares at the arctic-blue walls. The song plods through her head, dolente.

Quando corpus / ··· Enter the alto ··· Quando corpus / Morietur /

The psychiatrist walks in and Amelia stands up to shake his hand. The floor lifts with major melodies. "I'm Dr. Stephens. Amelia . . . I know, I've heard all about you."

"Have you?" she asks, seeking solace in cellos. Dr. Stephens sits behind the desk and looks through the file he brought in with him.

"Amelia Adams . . . very interesting. I've studied your file and staff reports, and we've come to the conclusion that all your symptoms are characteristic of bipolar two disorder."

Amelia rolls her eyes. "I've said this a million times: I never get happy. I get agitated, not 'manic.'"

"Bipolar two disorder has exactly that distinction from bipolar one: hypo-mania. That's the difference."

Fac, ut animae donetur /

Dr. Stephens takes out a piece of paper. He draws a horizontal line straight across the middle, then a heartbeat pattern up and down over the line, as the duet polarizes.

Paradisi gloria /

"This is bipolar ONE," he says, referring to the paper. "Euphoric high, crash, neutral, euphoria, crash, et cetera." He takes out a red marker and draws the same heartbeats well below the line. The soprano complements. The doctor continues, "This is bipolar TWO: suicidal, aggressive, high energy, which we call 'hypomania,' crash, depression, dysphoric hypomania, and so on. You never get up to neutral or have a euphoric high like type one. This disorder is a disability, and we're taking it very seriously. You need aggressive psychopharmaceutical treatment."

"Crazy pills," Chris's voice echoes in her head.

"This is not something to scoff at," he says sternly. "You can have a healthy life without thoughts of suicide. You can have a steady job, and stable relationships. If you get on board and take the medicine."

Amelia is distracted by the song, and confused by the news. "I just don't . . . I just don't know anything about it! I've never even HEARD of it!"

Dr. Stephens pulls out a thick, hardcover copy of the *DSM-IV*, turns to the section on bipolar two disorder, and slides it to her across the desk.

Morietur /

What she hears is a coagulation of energies like bees smothering in their own honey. She could dry the song out, put it in a rock tumbler, and place the shining specimen in a curio cabinet to awe and admire. Be sure to flip the safety.

"Amelia," the doctor starts, "Your disorder is a chronic illness, with few periods of stability between episodes. It is often misdiagnosed because people usually come in when they're depressed—not when they're hypomanic like you are now."

Amelia inhales the harmony: *Fac, ut animae donetur /*

"Bipolar two is not just a milder version of bipolar one. It actually has a higher suicide rate," he continues. "Fifteen to twenty percent completed. Attempted higher. The only mental illness deadlier than bipolar two is anorexia. Your complete diagnosis is bipolar: type two, hypomanic (dysphoric), severe with psychotic features."

Paradisi gloria /

"Psychosis is somewhat rare in bipolar two; usually that lands you an automatic bipolar one or schizoaffective, but I've considered your symptoms and I think the TWO diagnosis is dead-on. The good news is that it can be treated. It must be treated, or you will eventually kill yourself successfully."

Amelia's eyes feel dry and cloudy, like glass marbles scoured by sand. "Death is the only thing I want," she says. "More than help, more than hope, more than healing or happiness or joy. I don't know why." *Slash the jugular. Extension cord noose* · · · **Baaaaaaann-nnnnggg.** Her body, smashed against the rocks of some California cliff. Trills.

Paradisi gloria /

"That means that your brain needs help to restore an optimum balance of neurotransmitters. That's what that means. Not that you're a bad person. Not that you are being punished. It's a flaw in chemistry, not character. Do you understand?" He appears to be genuine.

Amelia's disappointment weighs heavy on her eyelashes. "I'm going to say I understand." *I'll just nick the jugular if this pill doesn't work. GET A FUCKING GUN!*

"Allow me to prove it to you," he offers. "The medicine I've chosen includes an antidepressant, a mood stabilizer, and an antipsychotic. And you will be continuing your Trazodone, so that's four."

Amelia is stunned. "FOUR? FOUR pills? Are you fucking

serious? Am I that crazy that I have to take FOUR pills?"

"Well, yes, in a sense." He leans against the desk. "Amelia, we hear you. We listen when you say you want to cut out your eyes, or starve yourself to death, or hurt others. That's why we're here: to listen. And to plan for the future. You need to take medicine to correct the chemicals in your brain. You have many symptoms to address, and therefore have to take more medication. We treat each symptom individually, so it requires more than one pill."

Amelia is in tears, grieving with the song until it turns into the "Amen."

Amen! /

FUCK YOU!

Amen! /

Fuck You, you evil bastard · · · **Amen!** /

"I'm going to give you these information packets—"

Torturer · · · **AMEN!** *MURDERER!*

"—and you are going to look through them."

Amen Amen Amen!

"You have the right to refuse treatment. Please let the nurse know what you decide by the end of the day."

Amen! You abandoned me! **Amen!** You gave me this curse! **Amen Amen Amen!** Amelia clutches the pamphlets and walks out of the office.

"Oh, and Amelia?" calls Dr. Stephens. She stops in the doorway and turns to him. She sees the sympathy in his eyes as he says, "I'm sorry."

> • Common side effects include nausea, vomiting, diarrhea, drowsiness, dizziness, tiredness, blurred vision, changes in weight, headache, muscle pain, dry mouth,

bad taste in the mouth, stuffy nose, constipation, or change in sexual interest.

- May cause the following symptoms: Anxiety, agitation, panic attacks, insomnia, irritability, hostility, aggressiveness, impulsivity, akathisia (psychomotor restlessness), hypomania, and mania.

- Families and caregivers of patients being treated with this medication should be alerted about the need to monitor patients for the emergence of agitation, irritability, unusual changes in behavior, as well as the presentation of suicidality, and to report such symptoms immediately to healthcare providers.

- A potentially fatal symptom complex sometimes referred to as Neuroleptic Malignant Syndrome (NMS) may occur with administration of this drug. Clinical manifestations of NMS are hyperpyrexia, muscle rigidity, altered mental status, and evidence of autonomic instability (irregular pulse or blood pressure, tachycardia, and cardiac dysrhythmia). Additional signs may include elevated creatine phosphokinase, myoglobinura (rhabdomyolysis), and acute renal failure.

- To relieve dry mouth, suck on (sugarless) hard candy or ice chips, chew (sugarless) gum, drink water, or use a saliva substitute.

- Tell your doctor right away if you have any serious side

effects, including shaking, tremors, nightmares, ringing in the ears, problems urinating, blood in urine, signs of infection (e.g., fever, persistent sore throat), shortness of breath, or stomach/abdominal pain.

- Tardive Dyskinesia: A syndrome of potentially irreversible, involuntary, dyskinetic movements may develop in patients undergoing treatment with this drug. There is no known treatment for established cases of Tardive Dyskinesia, although the syndrome may remit, partially or completely, if treatment is discontinued.

- Hyperglycemia and diabetes mellitus have been reported in patients treated with this drug, in some cases extreme and associated with ketoacidosis, hyperosmolar coma, or death.

- Remember that your doctor has prescribed this medication because he or she has judged that the benefit to you is greater than the risk of side effects.

GENESIS

Amelia stands at the nurses' station at 9 p.m. while Pantera picks "Floods" at sores in her mind. When it's her turn, she nervously accepts what the nurse gives her, stares at the four pills, takes them, and goes to bed, dragging the song with her.

When she gets into bed, her mind perseverates on graphic images of violence. Sawbone hambone. The axe bites deep into the back of her knee and she can feel the metal grinding against the bone. Mutilated bodies of dead children, burnt crosses, and a dog with its mouth wired shut. Corpses on marionette strings, dancing along with the music. The song continues while she imagines every way in which she could be tortured. How many times can you think about the same injury? The same hot blood and the same splintered bones, the same teeth through the tongue and smashed jaw, whiplash grotesque and always horrifying, but the same.

Amelia wakes up and vomits all over the bed. Jesus, nailed to the cross. She pulls off her gown and crawls into the shower. A high-pitched voice calls to her, as she pushes the shower button ::A TWENTY-MINUTE ETERNITY:: Her hand slams into the wall again ::A TWENTY-MINUTE ETERNITY:: The warm water rains down with the voice ::A THOUSAND LIFETIMES:: *Drown them. Drown them all.*

Her eyes open at dawn. A figure is wiping the waterproof mattress down with Lysol. The woman puts on a fresh blanket and pillow, then drags Amelia out of the shower. The orderly towels her off, coaxes Amelia into a clean hospital gown, and tucks her into bed.

Amelia passes out. She dreams about being forced to smash Blue's head in with a rock. His eyes are confused but trusting. It takes five attempts.

An orderly brings breakfast and wraps Amelia's arms in dry gauze while the song haunts her. She eats some toast, but when it's time to take the pills, Amelia gags on them, then blacks out as Paul Anselmo's voice spirals into the abyss at measure fifty-four.

She wakes up on the shower floor. There are the bubbles of saliva · · · Pink, flecked with blood from when she tried to choke out her powerless words of fear · · · Drowning in fury. There is the small bruise by the nipple, sweet like a smear of plum, roughly the size of a finger pad and unlikely to heal under the hard skin. Yes, perhaps it IS all in the details. *Drown us. Drown us all.*

An orderly is speaking to her but Amelia can't understand the words.

"Are you having hot flashes?"

All she can hear is the voice from the song.

"Goosebumps when you're not cold?"

Is she asking me a question? Someone checks her vitals before giving her food. The high voice makes promises. Amelia vomits again. *Drown her. Drown them all.* The orderlies clean up and tuck her back in. Pantera burrows in her brain like a parasite. Amelia crawls back into her tomb and hits the shower button over and over and over again.

The Lord saw that the wickedness of humankind was great in the earth—she tears off her wet bandages—*and that every inclination of the thoughts of their hearts was only evil continually. And the Lord was sorry that He had made humankind on the earth, and it grieved Him to His heart. So the Lord said, 'I will blot out from the earth mankind . . . For I am sorry that I have made them.'*

Anselmo's voice splits in two, then three, spreading toward consonance like a speculum. Amelia crawls back into the shower and turns it on, still wearing her hospital gown. Faces float past her eyes, the room tilts, and she runs back to the toilet to puke again. *Die Die Die Die* / **The mon-key chased the wea-sel** / runnerut, runnerut, runnerut, runnerut, runnerut. More vomit comes pouring from her mouth. She thinks of the clown instead of the clear bile in the toilet. *DIE DIE DIE DIE* / **The mon-key chased the wea-sel** / runnerut, runnerut, runnerut, runnerut. For days, Amelia lies on the shower floor while Dimebag Darrell solos.

My brain is in the press. They are taking all of me that is liquid until I am left watching baby cartoons on mute because *Jeopardy!* is overstimulating. Chemical lobotomy. Leave me clutching the dry paste of brain matter like poi, like Communion, like spackle that will later harden like concrete like asphalt like stone, crystallize my brain cells. They are SQUEEZING me to suck out the nutrients that make me blaze. Extinguished. They are kicking in my belly like some ungodly (literally) fetuses twisting up my intestines, wrapping them neatly around tiny vicious toes and stubs of newly grown fingers like telephone cords, then yanked. There are a thousand of us in this box that is getting smaller and smaller and we can't escape.

"She shows no sign of serotonin syndrome or shock."

A Middle Eastern woman screams and pleads, tearing at her long, beautiful hair. Begging. She is trapped in a 10 x 30 x 10 foot cube. Above her is a thirty-million gallon tank of water held at bay only by a single pane of glass. It creaks. Groans. And she screams (they panic).

"Pupil dilation normal."

I want to die in the worst way. I want to feel all my spongy parts. I want to lick the abscesses of pain, those fissures in my soul that are unfathomable, unreachable. Burning in their graves; silent in the grey. Look at the pinkness, the depth of the wound pulling tight and in and down like it could suck in my whole arm, consuming like so many mouths, like sea anemones. Charlie, help me. Somebody help me ::GLARES ALL AROUND:: Well if it isn't Smokey the Fucking Bear. Helpme McHelperson. They smother her. The kindergarteners dance on her grave as she decomposes in fast-forward.

She scrambles out of the shower to throw up again, and vomits so hard that her contacts fold up in her eyes. *DIE DIE DIE DIE* / **The mon-key chased the wea-sel** / runnerut, runnerut, runnerut, runnerut, runnerut, runnerut. The orderlies give her food. *DIE DIE DIE DIE* / **The mon-key chased the wea-sel** / runnerut, runnerut, runnerut, runnerut, runnerut, runnerut, runnerut, drums · · · She pukes it all up, her tear ducts finally flushing the little plastic discs from her sticky eyelashes into the yellow pool beneath her chin. **Pop! goes the wea-sel.**

She lies in the shower, getting out only to vomit. The orderlies feed her on the wet floor when the water turns off as lightning stabs her corneas. **BANG BANG BANG BANG BANG BANG!** *LET US IN! Jack-in-the-box.* They check her stool for blood. She chokes down more pills, crying. They are CRYING. They are all crying. It is muted as though there is a barrier between Amelia and her mind. **BANG BANG BANG BANG BANG BANG!** *LET US OUT!* They are banging and screaming and shouting · · · Wailing to be allowed back into her presence? Existence? Acknowledgment? I feel sorry for them. For me.

This time, she doesn't even get out to throw up. The frothy pill foam washes down the drain as she retches directly over it, like pearls dissolved in vinegar. She slams her fist against the metal protrusion **BANG BANG BANG BANG BANG BANG!** demanding more water. *Let us out! Let us in! Let us out!* **BANG BANG BANG BANG BANG BANG!** *Drown us all. We all deserve to die.* Thunder crashes in her head as the guitar fades out. The music stops and changes from the song to the sound of water on the linoleum floor.

PART II

REVELATION

Two of the holes in the showerhead have uneven pressure and are combining to make one thick stream dripping down onto Amelia's arm ::SILENCE:: The water receding from the faucet pats on her skin · · · Syncopated. Her eyes open and focus on the tiny flecks of brown in the beige linoleum of the shower floor, then ten feet across the bathroom to where an orderly sits in a chair with a clipboard. How long has she been here? The woman's eyes are set deep into her brow, and the whites are slightly yellowed. How long have I been here? Her skin is the same color as Amelia's mahogany piano when it has been freshly oiled. The creases in the woman's uniform crash together when she stands to help Amelia out of the shower.

"You alright there?" the woman asks, stooping down with a towel.

Amelia can smell cigarettes on her.

"You've had a rough week. Let's get you up and moving."

She hoists Amelia up like a bedraggled cat, and places the scratchy towel on her shoulders. The orderly's voice resonates in her bronchial tubes while she holds open Amelia's safety gown. "Pretty soon you'll be out of this thing and into some real clothes." She fastens the Velcro. "Sit down on the bed, here." The sheet crackles under Amelia's thin, wet thighs. Safety dressed in a pattern of delicate ivy that someone, somewhere thought would be soothing. The orderly checks her pupils with a flashlight. "Good." She turns off the light and asks, "Do you still feel nauseous? Dizzy? Confused?"

Amelia shakes her head.

"Put your hands out in front of you like this."

Amelia holds out her arms, palms down, and the woman smiles a sepia grin. "No dyskenisia, that's good. Your stitches need to be looked at, though, they're not supposed to soak in water like that." She makes some notes on her clipboard, then takes a long look at Amelia's haggard face ::SILENCE:: "You check out okay. But you need to be completely honest with the doctor and nurses about your side effects. If at any time you feel disoriented, shaky, or can't stop moving, tell someone immediately. And let us know if you get any kind of rash, that's a bad sign." The woman's dark eyes appear full of concern. "I'm going out to help with lunch. Come eat when you're ready, you've got to be starving." She smiles again and leaves Amelia alone in her room.

There is a conspicuous lack of music. Everything is visually stable but blurry at about a few yards due to her ejected contact lenses. Amelia touches the white-and-green sheet. Might as well be a vinyl tablecloth. She goes to the recessed shelves to find her slipper socks, and sees that the wood is real pine, not a facade glued on or particleboard. Clean and buttery, the walls are not tan but a very pale yellow. The HVAC system wheezes and gives a shudder in the ceiling, and for a brief moment, Amelia is filled with hope that the entire building will come crashing down on her, but the sound persists without any physical incident and Amelia is distracted by another thought.

My arms hurt.

She studies the swollen, waterlogged wounds attached to her. They ache on the inside ::SILENCE WHILE THE PAIN EXISTS:: There is another ache. In her stomach. A hollowness. It propels her out of the quiet, toward the promise of food in the common room. Her gown shears her ears with sound as she moves, and the Velcro tabs claw at her skin. She can feel every split end in her soggy hair when she steps into the bright hallway.

Amelia squints at the fluorescent lights that reveal fingerprint smudges on the light blue paint at waist-level and shoe grime on the baseboards. The rubber bottoms of her safety slippers against the floor make a whispering sound like peeling Scotch tape off a windowpane. The roar of lunch gets louder with each step, until someone yells at her.

"Look who's up! The orderly told me—" The stranger's eyes widen at the flesh pushing against Amelia's stitches. "—that you need a wrap, so if you'll just sit down in here."

The lady's scrubs are covered in Disney cartoon characters. Amelia braces herself for the inevitable assault of "It's a Small You-Know-What."

::SILENCE::

"I'll get some Silvidine; those look awfully red after all that exposure. Yes, wait here, Amelia."

Who the hell is this bitch? How does she even know my name?

The office is little more than a closet with two chairs, and a row of medical supply cabinets on one side. The walls are bare, with a patch where the doorknob hits the drywall. Her stitches pinch and rip at the edges like rows of fingernails torn from their beds. Tick. Tick. Tick. Amelia rolls her eyes. Of fucking course. A clock. She takes the clock off the wall, removes the batteries, and trashes them.

::SILENCE::

The woman returns with the ointment, gets bandaging supplies from the cabinets, and smiles. "Let's get you wrapped up so you can have lunch. I bet you're hungry after all that vomiting, huh?" she asks jovially.

Amelia stares at her. She has untrustworthy teeth. "I threw up so hard my contacts came out."

"Yes, I mean, apparently they're serving a side of fresh fruit salad. That sounds nice, doesn't it?"

Amelia doesn't answer. Too straight. Too white. Her eyes are that disturbing shade of blue that light contacts cast over brown irises. Makeup sinks into her pores. Coquinas in the tide.

The woman begins tapping the silvery cream onto her arm and Amelia winces. "When did this come loose?" asks the woman, indicating a stray stitch.

"I don't know. Sometime in the shower."

"Well you need to have it redone," the lady says.

Amelia notes the dark roots inching from her scalp and wonders if her tits are fake, too. "I don't want it redone. I'm not letting that stupid bitch touch me ever again."

"What, you don't like Rhonda?"

"She told me God would heal me if I truly repented. And she stitched me without anesthetic," Amelia says with a blank face.

The woman is skeptical. "Why would she do that?"

"To teach me a lesson. To punish me. I don't know. I just don't want her within arms' reach the rest of the time I'm here."

"Yes, well, no one else is qualified to do that," says the blonde.

Amelia's eyes narrow. "Are you telling me that, in this entire ward, there is no one else QUALIFIED to sew up my arm?" The woman purses her sticky lips. "No one else? Not one single person? What about you? Are you QUALIFIED?"

"No, I'm just an intern," she apologizes. "Wrapping your arms up is about the extent of what I'm allowed to do. I just wanted to meet you because Daniel said you were interesting."

Oh for fuck's sake. "Please don't use that word to describe me."

"Oh, okay sorry," the useless intern offers an apology. "Well, look . . . the God stuff . . . they don't mean it literally. It's just another way of saying, 'I hope you feel better soon.' You shouldn't be offended."

"I know. I'm not exactly offended, I'm more . . . guilty. It makes me feel guilty."

The intern pats her leg. It feels like rape. "Yes, well, I'm sorry if anyone has made you feel guilty."

"Thanks." Amelia's stomach growls.

The useless intern poorly secures the gauze on Amelia's left forearm and smiles. The mouth is full of razorblades. "We're all done here, and just in time to eat. It was nice to meet you. Enjoy that fruit salad!" She pushes Amelia out into the noise, before adding, "Oh, and my name is Heather, by the way."

Amelia doesn't turn to look back.

I hope I disappointed you.

THE BOOK OF NOISE

With her blurry vision, Amelia hears more of the common room than she sees: twelve mouths chewing, teeth grinding down feed like goats at a petting zoo. Juanita's choking protest when Maxwell steals her drink. Charlie usually sits in the back left corner. She makes her way to him through the cacophony. Maxwell takes notice.

"Hey everybody look! She's baa-ack!" He sidles up to her, close enough that she can see him clearly. He has grey shark eyes and acne scars across his cheeks. "They got you all drugged up now, don't they?" He reeks of cigarettes. Does every person in this place smoke? "Is the world suddenly bright and beautiful? Have all your problems gone away? Are you shitting rainbows and starshine?" He bear-hugs Amelia, then viciously twists her arm. "INDIAN BURN!"

"Max, you fucking psycho, what the fuck?"

He scampers away. Pain radiates from her elbow to her fingertips.

"Nice to see you back in reality, Amelia," says Daniel, offering her a tray of food. His voice is deep and smooth like that because he's tall, and his vocal chords are thicker. "Fresh fruit salad, made by the ladies at St. Thomas Episcopal Church." His whole vocal apparatus is larger. She looks at the jugular pulsing inches from his Adam's apple and takes the tray. "Oh look! Your boyfriend is here."

Amelia squints at a figure moving toward her. It appears to be stumbling.

"Aw, he's happy to see you!" Daniel intercepts Jackoff just as he comes into focus: naked from the waist down with a full erection.

"Hey!" calls Charlie. "Amelia!"

She follows the movement of a hand waving, and finds him sitting in the back left corner. Amelia slides her tray onto the table and sits.

"Hello, my friend," Charlie smiles. "Welcome back." The edges of his teeth are rounded from stomach acid.

"Thanks." *Jack-in-the-box.*

"How bad was it? Your roommate complained the whole time about not getting to use the bathroom." Charlie's broad, bony shoulders prod the seams of his designer shirt.

"Bad enough that I completely forgot I had a roommate." I can feel every split end, every ragged cuticle, the liquid in my brain between the spongy grey matter. My head is ringing with noise and my eyebrows are coming out. My eyelashes are falling out. "Most of it was either throwing up or trying not to throw up."

"Yeah, you definitely broke some blood vessels in your eyes." Now they look like yours—only hazel instead of blue. "I wanted to bring you flowers, like last time, but that bitch nurse says I can't give you potentially dangerous items."

"I wouldn't have noticed it anyway. It was like the worst case of the spins you've ever had."

"Weed before beer, everything's clear," Charlie quips. "Beer first and weed's the worst."

"For sure." Amelia sniffs at her food. Her mouth is watering, but she can't tell if it's from hunger or the need to vomit again. "I don't even know what day it is."

"It's Wednesday. Nice of them to have the fruit salad."

Amelia stares at the impossibly bright strawberries; golden peaches; fat, split grapes; and glistening mandarin oranges ::SILENCE:: She cautiously loads half a strawberry onto her plastic utensil, then puts it in her mouth. 4th of July · · · Flag cake. Sparklers writing swear words in the night. The flavor is almost too intense to bear.

"These strawberries are really sour." The joint between her skull and mandible puckers and pinches her. "What about this rice? This rice looks pretty good." Amelia scoops a sporkful of rice into her mouth. Fields upon fields of rice and grain. Bare, wet feet. "I can totally taste this!" Children laughing on brightly colored boats. She gets another mouthful in before she's done chewing the first. "What's IN this?"

"It's rice, Amelia. It probably came from a box. It doesn't even have butter on it."

"It doesn't need butter." Her saliva carries all kinds of messages from her tongue to her brain. This is good for you. Nourishing.

"Rice is notoriously hard to purge," Charlie chides her.

"Fuck that," says Amelia, maneuvering lukewarm, soupy canned corn onto the spork. "I've puked enough for a lifetime." Each kernel crunches and bursts in her mouth. Heat and sun and tall, leafy plants. "The pharmaceutical consultant said my major side effects would last a week or two, and would taper off after that." Amelia is ravenous. Generations of rewarding toil. Charlie stares in shock as she shovels the corn into her mouth, barely chewing. The fields are green and rolling.

"Are you being serious right now?" Amelia doesn't stop until the rice and corn are gone. She tries a piece of chicken thigh, wet death, and spits it back out onto her tray immediately. He waits until she goes back to the fruit cup to ask her. "Do you still want to die?"

Her hand stops in midair ::SILENCE:: She searches her mind for an answer, but it does not come easily. "Yes. But not in a suicidal sort of way—in an existential way. I mean, I don't want to KILL myself anymore, but I still want to die. Does that make sense?"

"I guess so. That's subtracting one level of violence."

"I want to die right now, pleased that I'd seen life and beauty and experienced it at all. And grateful, I think." The peach tastes like bright sunlight and ribbons. "Dying would be letting go of ALL—all of the bad AND all of the good. Just to be grateful for fire and Salvador Dalí, the ocean and true love. To quietly accept famine, pollution, cancer, and terrorism. That's why I want to die right now, because I understand that, and just understanding it is enough. I don't have to enjoy it to appreciate it." Amelia savors a mandarin orange that tastes like that time she went to Cancun on spring break, then gestures with the prongs of her spork toward the rest of the room. "I never thought it would be so noisy, though."

"What do you mean noisy?" Charlie's eyebrows are a darker shade of brown than his messy hair. "The common room is always noisy."

"I mean little things. Your chewing, the fluorescent lights, the clock on the wall, a dozen mentally ill people stuffing their faces—it's deafening." Charlie's face drops.

"You can hear me chewing?"

Fear dilates his pupils. Shit.

"Yeah, not like a slob or anything, but I can hear it."

Tears well up in Charlie's eyes, and he excuses himself. Goddamnit.

Amelia stares at her plate, with nothing to help her manage her guilt but a cold, greasy piece of chicken.

::SILENCE::

166

THE BOOK OF SILENCE

Amelia walks into the lemon-scented group therapy room late. Charlie, Marvin, Pedro, Maxwell, Juanita, Rosemary, and Susanna already sit in a circle of flimsy plastic chairs. There are pastel construction paper garlands and Easter-themed posters all over. Time for my Mensa meeting. Nurse Jessica stands when she enters.

"Welcome back, Amelia." She gestures to the place Charlie has saved for her. "I understand you've had some side effects, so it's nice to have you back in Group again."

"Thanks, I'm feeling better." Amelia slides in next to Charlie. Nurse Jessica has Disney princess eyes.

"Are you sure you wouldn't like to join us in prayer today?"

"No . . ." Amelia contracts the tops of the muscles above the apples of her cheeks. "I can't force myself to believe any of that. A real god would not tell you to hate yourself for imaginary infractions, or that you are guilty from birth, or that both a white lie and genocide deserve the same sentence. There is only law and chaos . . . and chaos is the fair one."

"If He doesn't exist, what's the harm in praying to Him, just in case?" asks Pedro.

Really? Pascal's wager?

"No omnipotent god would be tricked by that little . . . scam. It's just . . . it's just a non-issue. God is dead. Rejoice, for you are free." The faces surrounding her are blank. Fuck it. "Besides, I don't really like sweaty hands and it's hot in here, so, no thank you, I appreciate your concern, but please know that it is entirely artificial. Go on then."

Nurse Jessica leads the group in prayer. This time, Amelia hears them. "Oh Heavenly Spirit, thank You for giving us this day to reflect on our pasts and futures. Thank You for having a plan to prosper us, and not to harm us." Her voice is pinched and nasal. I wonder why I never noticed that before. Such an unfortunate voice for such a pretty face. "We ask Your blessing of hope and insight for the time we are gathered together, and from this moment forward. For You renew us in mind and spirit, and we put our trust in You. Amen."

::BLESSED BLESSED SILENCE::

"We haven't heard from Amelia in awhile, so I would like to give her the opportunity to discuss her experience of starting a journey to healing. Please raise your hand if that is unacceptable to you."

Maxwell raises his hand as if he has suddenly had an idea for mischief. "I wanna be excused."

"That is your right," she allows, and Maxwell runs off.

"And me," croaks Rosemary through half a century of tar and ash in her lungs. "I have to go wash my vagina." Rosemary is dismissed with a nod.

"Anyone else? Amelia, are you comfortable with this? I don't mean to put you on the spot if you're not ready."

"Yeah, sure," Amelia shrugs ::SILENCE:: The group waits for her to begin ::SILENCE:: "Well . . . I think I'm starting to put it together . . ." She struggles for the first time in her life to find the right words. "I feel a little bit better and a little bit worse. Better in that I can feel SOMETHING, but worse in that . . . well, that's just what comes along with being able to feel." ::SILENCE:: "I think the most distressing thing about my new medication is that it is silent in my head. It's lonely. I mean, I can think more clearly now, but

I'm a lone perspective. I'm like a diamond that has not yet been cut; I have only a singular, jagged face. And it is the most boring thing ever." I don't know if it's worth it. "I miss my friends—the voices, I mean, and even the ones that were my enemies. I miss Chopin's 'Nocturne in E♭.'" She fails to conjure it in her head. "It's very difficult to separate myself from music. I must always invest some portion of myself into listening and relating. But now, I have no way to relate to the world. It's just silence."

Charlie purses his lips around his damaged teeth. "You don't hear music anymore?"

Amelia listens to the silence. No. "No. There's no music." There's no music.

"Are you feeling better though?" asks Pedro. He is beginning to grow a wispy mustache below his oily nose.

"I don't know. I feel less suicidal, which is a relief, but . . . I used to feel as if I were sitting in a room amongst all of the knowledge I contain. Every song I've ever memorized and every thought, so many thoughts that could swoop in at any moment; they could float down from the heavens and alight on me like the most unexpected of gifts. And now I am separated from that. I feel like I don't know anything. I can't think unless someone asks me a question. It's disturbing without the music. All the silence and noise." ::SILENCE:: "Music was my best and most reliable companion. And now it's gone. It's all gone."

"What about the positive effects?" encourages the nurse.

"Well, like I said, I feel less depressed. Like I might start looking before I cross the street."

Nurse Jessica nods. "That's a start. What else?"

"Colors are much . . . brighter." Amelia struggles to put it into words. "Everything looks . . . exaggerated. And the food . . ." Amelia straightens, takes a deep breath, and exhales quickly. "I don't know how to describe it. There aren't words."

"Is there anything else you'd like to share?" she asks.

Amelia shakes her head, painfully aware of the weight of her hair.

"Are there any questions for Amelia?"

Marvin raises his hand. "Do you still want to kill yourself?"

"No." I haven't thought about cutting out my eyes once since I got up. She searches her mind. "But I do hope that I'll die soon, from a car accident, or electrocution, or being murdered by a gang—anything is fine, as long as my conscious existence ends."

"If you're not feeling suicidal, why do you still want to die?" he pushes.

Because I'm spiritually deformed. Because of the unbearable greatness of being. Because it won't last. "Habit."

"That's a very good question, Marvin, and an interesting response from Amelia. We all have habits that are maladaptive. Maybe we'll do collages on that, next session."

Collages. Amelia rolls her eyes. Why not a diorama?

"You seem a lot less angry," offers Pedro.

"Yeah, I feel free, in a way. Like taking a deep breath after almost drowning. The whole concept of punishment has been shifted off my shoulders. All I needed was medicine. I don't even have to consider guilt or shame, or sin or forgiveness. Plus, it got rid of the hymns I've memorized over the years. Those play in my head all the time. Especially in the morning." ::SILENCE:: "Used to play. Now it's just the noise of reality. I don't know which is worse."

Pedro nods his greasy head in understanding, and continues along her line of thought. "I know how you feel. When I started my antipsychotic, I lost my best friend. They said she wasn't real, but she was always there for me, no matter what. Then I . . . I killed her. With these pills. I poisoned her to death, and I've never been lonelier in my life! And I still have to deal with these fucking germs! These germs all over the place, crawling in and out of my head and no one to comfort me!"

"Pedro," the nurse holds up her hand, "I would like you to take a deep breath and—"

Fear and anger lift him from his seat. His words are pointed at Amelia. "Don't you think I miss her? How am I going to live with these meds if it means I lose her? 'Take your pills! Take your pills! Poison yourself with this shit.' NEVER HEAR MUSIC AGAIN! IS THAT WHAT YOU WANT?"

Never hear music again. Never hear music again. Never hear music again. Daniel and two other orderlies appear behind Pedro, telling him to relax. He keeps yelling, then starts thrashing around in anger. The sound of flesh grappling flesh is damp.

"If you can't calm down, we're gonna have to take you down," warns Daniel.

Pedro bores his plain brown eyes, made spectacular with rage, into Amelia's face and screams, "NEVER HEAR IT AGAIN!" The cry pierces her eardrums. The other orderlies hold Pedro as Daniel injects the young man with Haloperidol. Never hear music again. The fight quickly goes out of him, and they lead him to an isolation room to calm down. Look at him. Like a docile calf. *That's you* · · · Chemical lobotomy.

The group is quiet. There's always a moment of silence after someone gets a Halo shot. Nurse Jessica quickly redirects the group's attention.

"Let's go around the circle and everyone say something positive to Amelia. We'll start with me and go to the left. I am glad to see you making progress. Marvin?"

"I'm sorry that you miss your music, but—" He rubs his balding head. "—I think it will change your life for the better."

"Juanita?"

Juanita makes a strangled sound. Amelia likes that Nurse Jessica asks her opinion, even though she is a mute.

"Susanna?"

Susanna's skin pulls across her hollow face like a night-ghast. "You usually have really pretty hair but it looks like shit right now."

"Something positive," Nurse Jessica frowns.

"Oh, okay . . ." Her ridiculous voice makes Amelia consider smiling despite herself. "I hope you fix your hair soon. Like, asap."

"Will do."

"Charlie?"

He looks at the floor, then into Amelia's strange amber eyes. "It looks like the YOU part of you survived." The nurse smiles at the patients. I think that's true. Amelia listens to the emptiness in her head, and finds one—a single, conscious voice.

Nurse Jessica clasps her hands together. "Very nice. I'd like you to break up into groups and discuss your own experiences with side effects."

Marvin, Charlie, Amelia, and Susanna huddle together. Charlie looks irritated.

"Goddamn I need a cigarette. Do you have any smokes, Susanna?"

"Yeah, I have like six packs behind the counter." She checks over her shoulder, then rolls her chair slightly further into the middle. "I stole matches."

Burn it. Burn it down.

"What? How?" whispers Charlie with an incredulous grin.

Burn us all.

"I waited for Rosemary to check them out, took them from her, and then she—" Susanna wobbles her grotesquely large head and exposes her speckled teeth in mockery. "—just couldn't find 'em!"

"This is why I missed you," says Charlie. The tip of his right index finger is scarred from stomach acid. "Let's go to the lounge as soon as this is over and request a good-behavior smoke. Candace always says yes. Marvin? Amelia?"

"I'm in," says Marvin.

NEVER HEAR MUSIC AGAIN! IS THAT WHAT YOU WANT? Pedro's voice rings in Amelia's head.

"I think I'm gonna take a shower." Her mouth is stinging with lemons, and the memory of her First Communion. Tears threaten her eyes.

"Well brush your fucking hair when you get out. You can borrow mine," Susanna chirps in her squeaky voice.

Charlie steps toward Amelia, all tenderness. "What's going on?"

"What if Pedro is right? What if I never hear music again? Is it gone forever? Am I poisoning myself into silence?"

"No. It's part of you. It's just . . . muted. For now." He looks into her pitiful face. "I'll come get you when our smoke break is over. I have an idea."

Then Nurse Jessica calls the group back together.

PSALMS

Amelia stands naked in the shower, fully aware of the orderly watching her from the seat in the corner. The clatter of water on the shower floor grates on her nerves. She closes her eyes and turns to the opposite wall for a moment of privacy.

So /

She prods.

::SILENCE::

So you think you can tell /

::SILENCE::

She tries something associated with a visual image.

The Simp-sons /

::SILENCE::

LAMB-Chop's play along /
This is the song that nev-er ends /
Jesus loves me, this I know /
Cuz Oscar Mayer has a way with B-O-L-O-G-N-A /

::SILENCE::

Amelia's face registers no expression; it is just as blank as her mind. How the hell am I going to live like this? "Can I have some shampoo?" The orderly tramples toward her with a small, white bottle, flicks it open with a snap, and squeezes a quarter-size dollop of unscented wash onto her palm. This is barely enough for half my hair, Amelia thinks, but does not complain. She emulsifies it in her hands and applies it to her roots.

It is not soothing.

After she rinses out the shampoo and wrings the water from her hair, the orderly offers her a small amount of conditioner, which Amelia applies to the dark ends only and does not rinse out. She is finished before the water turns off. The orderly's sensible non-slip shoes squeal against the linoleum like sound check feedback when she gets Amelia's towel, which is thin and merciless against her skin. Every thread tears at her flesh. All her nerves are attached to one another so that drying off her left leg can be felt in the back of her throat. Amelia's eyes water at the sight of the safety gown.

The woman sighs with apology. "Everyone hates these things." She fastens the Velcro. "But better safe than sorry. I bet you'll get approved for clothes in no time." The auburn woman has kind, warm brown eyes and an abundance of light freckles. "There."

Amelia starts to lose her composure. Never have I felt like such a freak. Never have I so deserved my humiliation. Her throat tightens as she nods and avoids eye contact when the orderly bids her goodbye. She sits on her bed and stares blankly at the wall. I am ashamed at my inability to enjoy life. It is disgusting to me that I don't. That I can't. It mortifies me that I'm not strong enough to do it myself, and that I have to go running to medication. I am ashamed of my scars. I am ashamed of the rest of me that is not yet scarred.

BURN US ALL.

THE GOSPEL OF CHARLIE

In the common room, Amelia sits quietly playing solitaire. Without a musical distraction, she thinks in disjointed phrases. Stupid solitaire ::SILENCE:: Gambit. Groundhog Day ::SILENCE::

Charlie suddenly appears. "I have a surprise for you," he grins. Amelia realizes she has lost her card game. To no opponent. FAILURE.

"I hope it's not more flowers because that cow will just throw them away again."

"I told you she'd steal your shit. No, this is better than flowers. It's clothes." Her eyes widen and focus on his cracked lips.

"Clothes?"

"I just got them approved by Daniel. Just a men's small T-shirt and boxers, but it's better than this," he says, touching the hem of Amelia's gown.

She cannot contain herself. "That . . . that's awesome Charlie. Thank you. Can we do that? Can we do that, like, now?"

"Yeah, just come with me," he says, and they sneak away.

The men's wing smells like the underside of a nutsack. I came this way during the fire drill, she thinks, remembering the flashing emergency lights. Some of the doors she thought were offices are actually single-occupancy rooms. I didn't know that was an option. He must have better insurance.

Charlie's room is completely different from Amelia's. The lights are incandescent, and he has a large dresser with knobs she can hang herself from and a twin bed with real sheets she can use as a noose. Amelia touches the cord to the lamp and wonders if she's wet enough to be electrocuted. Charlie motions for her to sit down on the bed while he checks the hallway, then shuts the door behind him ::SILENCE::

Amelia sits with her knees folded under her, enervated. Her hair is wet and tangled. Her face hollow, pupils dilated in the dim light, collarbones sharp underneath the pathetic piece of cloth she wears to identify her as dangerous.

"You're starting to feel like a human, so you should also look like one," says Charlie, taking a plastic comb from the sturdy, square-corner dresser she can hang herself on.

Human. The word thrums through her like an arrow. Pieces of her heart cling to the fletching. He kneels behind Amelia on the bed, and gently starts loosening the knots in her hair. It takes a long time; her hair hasn't been brushed since her first night of medication. Amelia relaxes as he cares for her in a way that has soothed her primate ancestors for millennia. The tangled hair transforms from disorder into long, even locks. They softly tickle her where the skin on her back is exposed. Human.

A muted acoustic guitar begins in her head, arpeggiated. What key is that? Charlie combs, Amelia listens F$^\sharp$ She can just hear it in the soft stretches of the back of her skull. What song is this? Maynard James Keens's charcoal voice begins singing in her ears. She only catches snippets as Charlie combs out knots. A Perfect Circle. "A Stranger." Why can I hear this? Amelia clings to it in desperation. Please. Please, please, please, she begs her brain, please let me have this. Let me have this one song. The violins and cellos swirl into their rivets like liquid cement, fastening the crickets into her head. A quiet ecstasy fills her. The drone of a bee funeral. An amalgamation of strings.

Charlie puts down the comb and goes to the dresser she can hang herself on, as the song continues. He holds up a GAP shirt and another with AIX emblazoned on it. "Which one?" he offers with a smile. The key that resonates behind her xyphoid process makes her say it · · · F#

"I want that one," she says, indicating the worn-in college wrestling shirt Charlie is wearing. He freezes. Amelia feels emotions showing in her eyes: acceptance, respect, trust. Human. Charlie takes off the shirt, and Amelia sees his eyes making emotions, too. Human. His body is as sleek and thin as the most glamorous rock star · · · Heroin chic. Human. Muscles gripping bone like skeleton scars, wringing candy burn striations across his chain-link stomach. A Perfect Circle feeds the yearning and helplessness and anonymity in her head.

Amelia doesn't say a word. She just looks at him while he forces himself not to obscure his nudity in front of her. And she sees. She sees the Jack-in-the-box, his bitter acid mouth, every post-holiday purge. She can see every act of self-hatred in the brain that manifests itself as Charlie. He is empty. Human. The strings caress his ribs as a cymbal shimmers discretely.

She stands up slowly and pulls off her gown. The sound of the strings protect her, rebounding across every hallway in Amelia's head, every dark corner and acoustic chamber, and it is like being naked in the presence of the real god: Man. No shame. No presumption. No vanity. Charlie beholds her. He is mach-3 and beyond the barrier. His eyes throb with the rhythm of her song, hurricane blue and gilded with pain.

They stand facing each other, flayed alive, as raw and exposed as frostbitten meat. Maynard whispers in her ear. A single piano note responds—a great boom, then another lonely *ping.* Charlie's eyes touch her face. They follow the clear indentation of the ribs in her chest. They stop at each self-inflicted burn scar marring the right side of her abdomen, thick welts of varying severity and age. They roam to her breasts, which are drooping with weight loss. Human.

Charlie then dresses her. His whip-thin arms cradle Amelia's waist, and guide her legs out from under her to lean back. It is a smooth and fluid motion, like the song. He makes love to her dignity. Kneeling at her feet, he admires the hollow between her hip bones, the way her pelvis strains at the skin. Charlie bows close and slides his shorts over Amelia's ankles, digging his elbows into the hard mattress for the chance to graze his cheek along her sharp shins. As he makes his way past her knees, he inhales the scent between her thighs in a deep breath. She smells like Fruit Stripe gum and espresso.

He slides up the real sheets she could hang herself with to slip a wiry arm into the space between her lower back and the bed, then lifts Amelia off her hips to gently pull the clothing up with his other hand. Her body responds when the material grazes the soft hair growing back between her legs. The more clothing she has on, the more their chemistry increases. Charlie places Amelia's bandaged arms into the old shirt one by one, so carefully, because he knows that what holds her together is not just stitches. The air between them changes. Human, she remembers.

Dynamic change: forte. The space between their mouths grows hot with tension. Charlie absorbs the chords vibrating in the blood under her soft skin, the thinness of her wrist bones, the loose stitch in the crook of her elbow, the smell of her body without artificial influence. Crescendo. She is almost dressed.

The siren tells her to shy away, run away, but she revolts against the lyrics. This is real. She breathes with the rhythm, and Charlie inhales every one of her sweet breaths like a smoke ring. They do not kiss. Fortissimo. Their hips join together as he pulls the shirt down her back, but he has no erection. Her nipples are soft and pink. They worship each other's unforgivable sins, and have soul orgasms.

The song is over. She is dressed again in clothes and silence. Charlie disentangles himself from her, and fixes a wisp of hair on her head. He looks straight into her eyes.

"Was that music?" Charlie whispers.

Amelia nods and chokes out, "Thank you."

GLUTTONY

Amelia, Charlie, Susanna, and Marvin sit around a table with their breakfasts in front of them. Amelia is adding sugar to her coffee. The smell of downtown Jacksonville. The dark liquid is too bitter for her chemically circumcised taste buds, so she adds a plastic thimble of cream. Marvin chews while Charlie and Susanna appear to be having a who-can-eat-less standoff.

Charlie looks across the room at John Doe and whispers, "He was definitely awake. He was saying no!"

"I heard him say, 'I don't want it,'" Susanna adds.

"Whether or not John Doe wants the shot is not the issue," adds Marvin. "Maybe he needs it as a safety precaution."

The powdered scrambled eggs have the texture of moist bread pudding. Amelia shovels peaks of sunny yellow into her mouth, adding a sporkful of hash browns here and there. Rounding up cattle bareback at sunrise. The lukewarm mixture tastes buttery and light. Gathering pecans at Aunt Cathy's ranch in the fall. The potatoes are crispy with grease. Saying 'pi-cahn' instead of 'pee-can' · · · 'You're just like your mother.' Amelia takes a sip of her milkshake coffee without Kelis stomping around her brain. It reminds her of her younger years spent writing in journals in a coffee shop by the beach, too young to appreciate the bold flavor but driven by artifice to drink it.

"All I'm saying," Charlie continues, "is he should have the right to refuse treatment, like everybody else."

"Ha!" squeaks Susanna. "They don't respect that shit. I tried to refuse a feeding tube and they shoved it in anyway."

"That saved your life!" Marvin's voice increases in volume and pitch. "Who's to say they're not saving his?" Amelia never cared for oranges because of their stringy webbing, but she tears this one apart, greedy for the sweet, bright flesh.

"Maybe he doesn't want to be saved," argues Charlie.

"Maybe it's not about saving him; maybe he's aggressive," Marvin counters.

Each section of the fruit gushes its juice over her tongue · · · Rivulets of vitamins and sunshine and fragrant blossoms in the spring. She thinks of the citrus trees in the backyard of her childhood home in Florida. Helping her father pick grapefruit · · · The smooth branches and sharp thorns. When the fruit is gone, she wipes her sticky fingers with the thin paper napkin. Desperate for any sort of pleasure, Amelia tips the Styrofoam plate toward her face and scoops the remaining globs of eggs and hash into her mouth. The material croaks between her hands. When she puts down the plate, she notices that the conversation has stopped.

Susanna hoists an eyebrow up her forehead with a look of disgust. "Amelia, what the fuck are you doing?"

"Eating," she mumbles. Charlie has a similar look on his face, but Marvin is smiling.

"No, you are FEEDING," Susanna corrects her. "Look at you. Like a dog in a fucking pizza box."

"I think it's great," says Marvin. "Finally putting some color in your cheeks."

"You're gonna get fat," Charlie says, as if the word is a cockroach on his tongue.

"REALLY fat," emphasizes Susanna. "Especially if you start drinking your coffee like that. FOUR sugar packets? Should I go ahead and get you some compression socks for your diabetes?"

Cut off the feet.

"Look, if food had always tasted this good, I never would've stopped eating in the first place. This shit is great."

"That's interesting," notes Marvin.

Amelia flinches.

"Your food tastes different?"

"It tastes . . . at all." She takes a sip of sweet coffee. "My jaw is actually tired from chewing so much."

Susanna rolls her decomposing eyes toward her receding hairline. "Why not just unhinge your jaw and swallow your tray whole?" She looks at Charlie. "Can she unhinge her jaw, Charlie?"

"I wouldn't know." He crosses his arms. "Maybe a slop bucket?"

"Look, I know you guys are into being skinny, but it was never about that for me. And now that I can taste my food . . . I never get to feel pleasure, and something so small, I mean, it's really good."

Susanna and Charlie sit, bemused, but Marvin is openly pleased. "I think you're the first person to ever say that about hospital food," he chuckles.

"Do you think that was a hallucination?" she wonders out loud.

"Delusion is the more appropriate term. That would make sense if you're on an AAP." Amelia turns her palms to the ceiling.

"Atypical antipsychotic," Marvin clarifies.

"Yeah, I'm taking one of those."

"And look what it's gotten you: a spectacular meal the rest of us take for granted."

"What a shame," Charlie shakes his head. "You're so fucking hot."

"Charlie, please," Susanna snorts, "Amelia is psych-ward hot, not real-life hot." She gives Amelia a long look of consideration before saying, "All right, well, from now on, you are responsible for making me look like I ate. I'm tired of hiding this shit in my clothes and they never give me enough napkins. I can 'accidentally' drop only so much, so from now on you have to eat it."

"Wait, wait wait. How much?" Amelia can smell death on Susanna's words as she leans forward.

"Half."

"Fuck you, half," Amelia scoffs. "I'm not eating half. I'm not actually trying to get fat, you know."

Fear flashes behind Susanna's crusty, rodent eyes. "One third. Or all the carbs."

"A quarter, of whatever I want," Amelia counters. "Plus your sugar and salt."

"Agreed."

"What's agreed?"

They turn to see Nurse Rhonda looming above their table. Charlie is the one who speaks. His eyes are pinhole cameras.

"Amelia's gonna get fat."

Nurse Rhonda shows her bleached teeth in a wicked grin, and her voice is deep as a viola.

"Aren't you all."

THE GOSPEL OF MARVIN

Marvin is sitting on the musty plaid couch in the common room, reading a newspaper with his back to the television when Amelia enters. Lucia and Maxwell are staring at the TV blaring *Bonanza*. At least it's better than the Catholic channel.

"Hey Marvin, have you seen Charlie?"

He doesn't look up from his newspaper.

"Charlie just saw the p-doc and is having a bit of a break-down. He's holed up somewhere, crying it out."

"Shit." ::SILENCE:: "Well, we usually play cards together, so now I don't have a partner. Do you want to play?"

He folds his newspaper expertly, and adjusts his glasses. "What are we playing?"

"Gin? Or whatever other game you want. I know speed, too."

A bug trapped in the overhead light flaps its wings desperately.

"The last time I played gin rummy was with my son during this big storm when the power went off," he says. "It brings back fond memories. Let's start with that."

They go to a rickety plastic table and Amelia shuffles the cards, relishing the feel between her fingers. The plastic has worn away from the edges, and they make a softer sound than a fresh pack.

"So, tell me about yourself, Marvin." The cards smell like old books.

"Well, I'm a family man. I'm a stockbroker. We live on the Gold Coast and have a Siamese cat my wife loves, but I think it has nefarious plans for me." Marvin smiles with substantial crow's feet radiating from his bright eyes. "I have a son, Gideon, who is six. I spend entirely too much time at work." Amelia deals the cards. "When I get depressed, I procrastinate and cry and miss out on time with my wife and son, but when I'm manic, man, I break the bank! Must be why they pay me so much."

Amelia is surprised. "Your mental illness helps you at work?"

"When the mania is on its way up, yes. I just feel so good. So alive! I shower my wife with diamonds and new cars, things like that. I take the Porsche out for the thrill of the speed. Everything is thrilling when you're manic; everything is an exquisite joy. But then you hit psychosis, and before you know it you're in the hospital. And here is NO work, NO wife, NO son, NO thrill."

"Why aren't you in one of those nice places?" Amelia speaks out of jealousy. Lucky. You should be grateful that you ever get to experience joy. "You live on the Gold Coast. It's not like you can't afford it."

"I'm not throwing my money away on something extravagant for myself when the bare minimum will do. The meds work, and I take them EXACTLY as prescribed, every day. If I start to go off-kilter while I'm on them, I just come in for an adjustment," he explains.

She looks at her faded cards, disappointed. "I didn't know adjustments were such a big deal."

"They are. You're talking about the balancing of neurotransmitters in the brain—the processing of an entire life experience. Even a little tweak can have big consequences in your ability to function. Hopefully, it causes a positive reaction, but the negative reactions happen, too."

So, what, I'm going to have to do this my whole life? Take this for that and that for this, until I'm so drugged up that finding myself is impossible? I don't know. He seems to be himself.

Marvin searches her face and frowns. "I hope they didn't damage you. Three new meds at the same time, that's dangerous. I heard them talking about serotonin poisoning."

"What's that?"

"Agitation, rapid heart rate, high blood pressure," he begins, a veteran of side effects. "Dilated pupils, tremors, muscle rigidity, hot flashes, sweating for no reason or getting goosebumps when you're not cold." He studies her more closely, gauging her pallor. "Seizures, heart attack, unconsciousness . . . death."

Amelia's face makes an involuntary twitch. Another chance to die · · · WASTED.

"I'm feeling better, though."

"You look better," Marvin relaxes his gaze. "Where'd you get the clothes?"

"From Charlie." Go to him. Go to him and help him. "I never thought such a minor thing could make such a difference. Clothes." Go to him and comfort him.

"That was nice of him." Marvin lays down a good set. "I think he has a crush on you."

Amelia's eyes snap up and catch in the reflection of the lenses protecting his eyes. "It's not a crush." A lyric from the Perfect Circle song suddenly appears in her thoughts, and disappears just as quickly as it arrived. "It's something, but it's not a crush." He lays down a hand ambivalently ::SILENCE::

"Marvin, what do you do when you get out of the psych ward?"

"I like to stay in a hotel for a week as a sort of transition back into scheduled life. Then I go home, call my boss, and go back to work," he says, matter-of-fact.

"They don't fire you for missing so much work?"

"First of all, it's not 'so much work.' This is only the third time this has happened in eight years, and it's just one month." Amelia wonders why he is still clean-shaven. "Second, they can't fire me for it because the ADA says they must make 'reasonable accommodations' for those with disabilities. Bipolar disorder is recognized as a disability, so I make reasonable requests for time off when I need it, and they accommodate."

Does he get razor privileges?

"That's pretty sweet," she says, losing.

"I think so," he nods. "It's a good life. I'm happy with my life. When I'm stable."

"And the qualities you've lost? The joy?"

"Yes, that. Well, sometimes I AM tempted to go chasing after that high, but then I remember that I've built myself a good life. And I derive joy from THAT. But I do feel . . . less brilliant."

So INTENSE, her father emphasizes in her head. She puts down a hand.

"That's sad."

Marvin raises his greying eyebrows and leans forward. "It's worth it," he assures her.

"Is it?"

She listens to the hum of electricity · · · Squealing dog operas emanating from every electrical device, high above the actual noise of mouth breathers and television.

Only one way to find out.

THE GOSPEL OF SUSANNA

Amelia walks into the smoking lounge, looking for Charlie. Her eyes flick to each blurry figure against the grungy, taupe wall. She can identify them by height: Rosemary, Maxwell, and Susanna.

"Where the fuck is Charlie?" she asks Susanna.

"Hell if I know," she replies in her comical, high-pitched tone. "I've been waiting for him or Marvin to come in and light my cigarette for me. I don't trust either of these psychos to not light me on fire."

"I gotcha," says Amelia, stepping into the hazy room. Susanna smells like death. This whole room smells like death. Amelia lights Susanna's cigarette, and does not consider burning herself with it.

"Thanks," she puffs.

"No problem." Amelia chooses to sit down instead of checking Charlie's room. She thinks if Death could choose a wife, he would surely love the sallow skin and stink of decomposition coming from Susanna as her body eats itself.

She searches her mind for something to say, but the frail young woman talks first. She sounds like Fievel.

"Amelia, what exactly is it that you have against cigarettes? Have you ever even tried one?"

Chris smoked. I always hated it.

"Never. I think I'd throw up if I did."

"How do you know you don't like them if you've never tried one?"

"I don't have to try herpes to know I don't want them," she

quotes her sister.

Susanna laughs in a bizarre hiccup. "You're waiting to die anyway, right? So what's the harm of one? Just try it." Susanna balances her cigarette between her thin, dry lips and uses her good hand to tap a Kamel Red onto her lap.

It's inoperable, says a doctor examining an X-ray in Amelia's head. *It started in the right lung, but now you can see it has spread to the lymph nodes. I'm afraid there's nothing we can do.*

"I'm not going to smoke a whole one, let me have a puff of yours."

Amelia reaches for the cigarette in Susanna's mouth, but she stops her. "I have HIV." Susanna's eyes are rat-brown and ashamed. "I don't know if you can get it from sharing a cigarette or not, but, better be safe."

::SILENCE:: "Yeah, thanks. Um, I'll just have that one then." ::SILENCE:: Amelia puts the yellow butt in her mouth, and is surprised that it tastes sweet. "Just . . . ?"

"Hold the lighter to the very tip, and suck with your lips."

Amelia does so, and holds the smoke in her mouth. Black barns in Kentucky. It's tangy and ashy, but not altogether unpleasant—like a Nazi knowing the snowflakes on his tongue are mingled with the ashes of cremated Jews.

"Now inhale through your mouth," instructs Susanna. Amelia inhales the smoke, and chokes on it. She coughs spastically while Susanna cheers and giggles. "I just took your nicotine virginity!"

"Gross," she gags. The drug hits her hard and she retches. Susanna's laughter rings in her head.

"Breathe, Amelia. Take in the good air and breathe out the smoke. You don't hold it in like weed."

Amelia gulps down the toxic air. Tar and feather the lungs. Crows using tools to get peanuts. Her head clears and her stomach settles. Think about the endgame. Susanna takes a drag. "You good?" Amelia nods. "Then finish it," she demands.

They sit in comfortable silence, smoking and gagging and coughing, both intent on death. As she becomes accustomed to the buzz building in her limbs, Amelia thinks, No one could blame it on me. I mean, it happens all the time. It's probably the best shot I have. She imagines her cremation. *Burn us all.*

When she's done with the cigarette, she puts it out, slips it into the bin, and looks at Susanna, whose eyes are rheumy around the eyelashes.

"Thanks."

"Thank YOU," replies Susanna, and Amelia leaves her there.

PROVERBS

Charlie, Marvin, and Amelia are early to group therapy. They stand near the door, engaged in conversation.

"Kierkegaard said that the failure of the self to relate to itself is the root of despair," challenges Marvin. He is relaxed and friendly, but Charlie bristles with some unnamable emotion.

"Then what saves me, if I can't relate to myself?" Amelia counters. "I don't have music to help me anymore. There is nothing to relate to, nothing to protect me from the assault of life on my senses or comfort me in my darkest places. There is only silence. If life is absurd and happiness really does evade me more specifically than others, then I am obligated by everything I believe to end my life."

"If you believe that life, nature, and the order of the universe are all absurd and chaotic, that has to leave room for the possibility of the existence of God. . . . For surely that would be THE most absurd phenomenon." He wiggles his eyebrows in good sportsmanship. "That puts a wrench in things."

"Then the most absurd thing that could possibly happen would be rational: healing. If I were healed, I'd have faith. How do I get faith?"

"The origin of faith is weakness of spirit. As they say in AA, you have to accept that you can't do it by yourself."

"I think the origin of faith is weakness of WILL. All the great religious figureheads—Jesus, Buddha, Mohammed—taught life-affirming practices in times of motivational desolation." *Kill the apostate*. "They try to strip away the virtues of strength and confidence in oneself, so that the will atrophies and the need to be commanded develops. Desperation for direction leads to more impotence of ambition, which craves still greater authority. You are a SLAVE, my friend." Marvin stiffens at this word, so she amends, "But whatever gets you through the day, man. The silence is fucking unbearable to me. Maybe it helps some people to fill it up with prayer."

"So what, you're gonna judge us now?" accuses Charlie, whose dark blue eyes are ringed in a betrayal that has nothing to do with her words.

"No, that's not what I meant." Why are his eyes like that? "I'm not angry or spiteful or bitter about it anymore. I'm just saying that religion is a construct meant to extend and increase proliferation of the species. It makes sense that those who break off from the masses, like me, often commit suicide. I no longer belong to that protective mechanism. Individualism is involution, devolution, or avolution— evolution away from the best interests of the species." She swats gnats from her mind. "Just ignore me. I'm making up words now."

The muscles between Charlie's jaw and ears tighten, and he exposes his throat to her before saying, "So you're more evolved than we are."

"No!" His eyes are swarming with debris. "Well . . . maybe? I don't know but it's not a GOOD thing. Don't you see? It might be true but it's not good." The APC song appears in her thoughts once more. Amelia shakes her head and searches the whirlpools in his face. "Charlie, come on," but Nurse Jessica appears with a rolling cart full of modeling clay.

"Charlie, are you okay?" the nurse asks between dimples.

Charlie cuts his eyes at Amelia. "Fine. Maxwell is in isolation right now. Daniel wanted me to tell you."

"Thank you, Charlie," she says as he walks inside to find a seat. Nurse Jessica turns her manga eyes toward Amelia and Marvin, who are caught in an uncomfortable silence. She observes them clinically for a moment.

"Marvin, may I speak to Amelia privately?" Other patients are filing in, and he merges into the queue. The nurse drops her entire persona, becoming sterile and stern. "I'm going to ask you not to mention religion any more in our discussions OR outside of Group to the other patients. You are seeding their minds with doubt and it's not healthy for anyone."

"You're the one always bringing it up! You pray before every session!" Amelia responds.

"Be that as it may, I will avoid the issue from now on, and I'm requesting that you do the same."

Look at her: complete moral authority.

Amelia chews a smirk off her lips and gives her a nod.

Nurse Jessica resumes her social-skills face, and says, "Thank you. Now let's put this behind us and make some ashtrays!"

ACTS

The art room is packed and humming, but fuzzy beyond her side of the table. Amelia considers the gentle cotton of Charlie's green boxers against her thighs as she paints in spectacular blues and purples with a real paintbrush. She does not think about stabbing her eyes out with it.

Marvin slides closer to Amelia and presses his closed fist against her hand. "I got you something." He slips a paperclip into her palm under the table.

"What's this for?" she whispers.

"You can play, right?" He subtly indicates the lock on the piano. "Wouldn't it help to, you know, MAKE the music? Then you wouldn't miss it so much."

Amelia stares at the cheap lock. Sheet music flicks through her head.

"As soon as she takes her bathroom break."

"Atta girl," he says. "You're welcome."

"Yes, thank you."

She pretends to focus on the painting, but her mind is racing. The songs are no longer bombarding her, vying for what gets heard, when. They come like predictable concentric circles in water around a dropped stone.

As the fat therapist approaches, Marvin says, in a much louder baritone, "Are you doing robots today?"

"No, I'm doing something different. Want to see?" Amelia holds up the painting. "It's a horse skele—"

The fat therapist snatches it out of her hands and cries, "A HORSE SKELETON! That is so INTERESTING! We're gonna have a field day with this one! Oh, and good for you for getting that robot thing under control. We were bored to death. You must be feeling better, drawing an animal, and the colors you used! Fascinating!" Amelia reaches out to get her painting back, but the fat therapist says, "Oh, actually, can I turn it in like this? My supervisor is gonna love it. I can just, take it, now, if that's—"

"Whatever. Take it." Her fingers are restless.

"I will! Thanks!" She rubs a hand over her big belly, and for the first time, it occurs to Amelia that she may be pregnant, accounting for her usual mid-session bathroom breaks. "Now if you'll excuse me, I need to use the restroom."

When the pregnant therapist leaves, Marvin and Amelia go straight to the piano. She fumbles with the lock.

"I can't do this! I don't know how!" she hisses to Marvin.

"I have a lock exactly like this on my toolbox. Let me try."

He rattles the paperclip around randomly until the lock clicks. The piano is open.

Amelia pulls out the wobbly bench and flexes her fingers. Debussy: "Suite bergamasque: Prélude," she orders her brain. She taps the lowest **F** with her left index finger, then touches the F an octave above to compare pitches. The notes scrape against one another in the air, off-pitch, but it sounds like salvation to Amelia. Rubato. She spreads her fingers wide to accommodate the bright first chord of the prelude and tests her finger pressure on the keys. The tendons in her arms are dry rubber bands that must be stretched carefully. Moderato. Her right hand clumsily pecks out the 16th notes before settling on the F^7 chord.

The room goes still.

The octaves boom again, with confidence. This time, all but her numb, right–middle fingers glide easily over the run, before the **C minor**. She sees the music in her mind. At measure eleven, she presses the keys harder. **2e+a3e AND a**. Decrescendo, then it waxes, then wanes, then waxes again.

Maxwell is caught in the tide. As if suspended from his shoulders from a meat hook, he leans forward and up at the same time. The muscles around his eyes relax. He puts his paintbrush neatly back into the basket before giving in completely.

A tempo: piano. A test of Amelia's dexterity, her left hand crosses over her right · · · Chord · · · Left crosses over her right · · · Mano sinistra, and back again. Lucia has gone completely silent. Amelia kneads the keys gently when the warm, pianissimo sharps come in. There is a strange, dull burn in her forearms. Her fingers climb the scale toward another round of delicate leaps across the keys. As the song gets softer, so does Rosemary's face · · · Drawn up like a used tissue, runny with tears and snot.

Molto pianissimo: stacatto. Amelia lounges on the rest.

Her left hand steps purposefully toward the deep end, moderato crescendo, with complete control, as her right hand builds chords at the top of the bass clef. She leans forward with the dictated waves to mezzo forte, then back. Adjusts her feet subconsciously to better grip the pedal with her socks. The hills come again, bigger and steeper. She ignores the dynamic markings here and hits the notes at forte with a slight ritardando, before moving into her favorite part of the piece.

Mano destra · · · Mano sinistra · · · Left hand crosses over the right time and again without error. Every accidental in place. Every patient transfixed. Every one of them an individual singularity, sucking sensation from near space; the music comes to them. Something small snaps in her right arm when she reaches the octaves at measure sixty. Amelia ignores it. Poco a poco crescendo. The flesh beneath her stitches protests. Sempre crescendo, toward a brilliant trill . . . and 32nds to the **G**! The knot in her sternum bursts open. Charlie covers his face with his hands, and tears pool in Susanna's wormy eyes.

Sfortzando! Debussy casts his opening measure again, then re-establishes piano in order to plant the low **C** that grows in 16ths. Lucia's lips tremble, but not in prayer. She is a silent, dark-eyed statue, burning with rapture. Amelia holds back, allowing the pressure, feeling the sensation. Molto crescendo: forte. Her fingers vibrate with the wooden box. Decrescendo, piu forte. Her wrists close in on each other for a measure, then her right hand flies up the keys again. Decrescendo, piu forte. She hits the broad chord with her thumbs nearly touching. Marcato marcato marcato! Her whole body is tense. Her hands grasp atoms in **F major**. The fluid in her cells resonates with the vibrations. Sempre marcato. And in bliss, just one more flight · · · Fortissimo · · · Suspended · · · Resolved · · · She dotes on the rallentando, then gives in to the root. After exactly four counts, she releases the pedal and the final chord rings through the room on the strength of her fingers alone. Lasciare suonare.

Amelia looks like she just got fucked by God, meek and limp and pulsing with aftershocks.

::SILENCE::

Dr. Stephens speaks from behind a crowd of orderlies at the door. "Amelia, I would like to see you in my office immediately."

"Okay." ::SILENCE::

"I'm going to have a discussion with my colleague here first," he says, as the pregnant therapist strokes her stomach nervously. "You know where it is. Wait there please."

"Sorry," she mumbles to the room, avoiding eye contact as she closes the piano and stands up. The old wooden bench squeals when she pushes it back into place. Amelia leaves without concern. What are they going to do, write me a referral? Send me to detention? She feels exorcised.

Dr. Stephens's door is open, and she picks the hard chair over the chaise ::SILENCE:: Tick. Tick. Tick. Her ears hone in on the clock. Tick ticktickticktickticktickticktickticktick. Her ears become so attuned to the relentless ticking that when Dr. Stephens enters, the door slams against the frame when he closes it. The expensive leather chair screams beneath him when he crashes into it · · · Polished nails wrenching against the stiff red skin. Tick. Tick. Tick.

He wrinkles his chin and leans across the massive desk, examining Amelia's face before saying, "How are you feeling? I know you were out for awhile with side effects, but how are you now that your body is adjusting?"

"Better I think . . ." She struggles to find the words. He just heard how I'm feeling. "Colors are so much brighter, and they're all so different from one another. At first I thought the medicine was triggering hallucinations, but now I can't tell if what I'm experiencing is a hallucination, or if I've been hallucinating for so long that reality comes to me as false or projective—as aggrandizement. And every time in the past that I believed I was hallucinating, I was really only having a break from my own delusional state to witness reality in itself. It's terrifying."

He nods noncommittally. "Do you still want to die?"

"Yes. Only not by my own hand. Hoping now for a good car accident or something else fortuitous."

"That's an improvement. What else has changed?"

Amelia rakes the desiccated garden in her mind. Tick. Tick.

Tick. "I feel sedated, but more like . . . myself. The ME me. But also guilty about locking away the voices and the music. I'm not hearing music at all."

"Guilty?" His forehead crinkles.

"Yes. For better or worse, I have always had music and different perspectives in my head. They have been my companions since I was twelve years old. Now, I've stuffed them into a cattle car on the way to a concentration camp, and the box is getting smaller and smaller every day." *LET US OUT!* "I'm abandoning them." *LET US IN!* "One day I might even forget them, which I want and also feel ashamed for. It was comfort and torture, and now it's so quiet, but loud. Does that make sense?"

"I'm not sure, but please continue."

I need my brain to describe this. I need those thoughts back. I need to know the soundtrack. Tick. Tick. Tick.

"It's like I'm hearing the world for the first time: the REAL world, with all its chatter and electronics and utensils scuttling across plates, and goddamn fucking clocks, and the sound of breathing. Did I ever breathe that hard? Have I been living in a disingenuous world for all this time, exchanging hard truth for mental distraction?"

"That's a good question. You're feeling confused about the remission of your psychosis. It's actually quite normal to feel a sense of loss for one's tormentors."

She thinks of Pedro's best friend.

"You said you feel more like yourself. What does that mean?"

Amelia tastes the words before saying them, displeased by their indelicacy. "Well, without the racing thoughts and continuous music, I feel like I'm more aware. That I know who I am. Even though I'm miserable and still looking forward to my life ending, I have a single, solid consciousness. And that's empowering."

"Good," says Dr. Stephens. He steeples his hairy fingers in front of his chest. "We are considering you for release."

Tick. Tick. Tick.

"How soon?"

"Monday at the latest." He scrutinizes her face. "You will be released into the care of your parents, return to Florida, and see a colleague of mine on an outpatient basis at the Mayo Clinic."

Mom will scream again. She may never stop screaming.

"We'll meet again before you go, to discuss your prognosis and answer any questions you may have."

Tick. Tick. Tick. The doctor continues, "Of course, we can't have you picking the lock on the piano. The art therapist said that you asked permission when you first arrived, and were expressly forbidden."

Amelia nods.

Dr. Stephens surprises her: "It was good."

"Yeah, sorry, I just—" Desperate for the possibility of playing again, Amelia fumbles for the words to say. "—Marvin suggested that since I'm not hearing music anymore, I need to MAKE it, outside of myself. Just even that one song made me feel . . ." ::SILENCE:: "It made me FEEL. And I think it was good for some of the other patients, too."

He nods in agreement. "That's exactly what I saw in there: utter and complete stillness. You know, I find your case interesting because I used to be a musician. I played the piano when I was younger, but stopped when I went to med school. I wish I had kept it up." He pauses. "So here's the deal: I have a box of sheet music in my garage. If you would like, I will bring it here and you can look through it. It's mostly classical. You get thirty minutes a day, under supervision, in the art room, at four o'clock. You do not let anyone else touch the piano. You do not let anyone touch the music. Deal?"

"Yes!" The response of the keys to her touch. The gentle, aching tugs of scar tissue. The smell of wood and strings and dust. "Yes, thank you, that is awesome. Thank you, oh my god, thank you!"

"You are more than welcome," he smiles. "I'll get it to you tomorrow."

1ST APOSTLES

In the smoking lounge after dinner, Charlie, Marvin, Susanna, and Pedro sit and smoke while Amelia listens. She glances at Charlie, who still refuses to look at her, then at the index card from Group stating how many times she has been hospitalized, and two things she wants to accomplish this time. Susanna is telling a funny story in her strange, mousy voice.

" . . . then my boyfriend slams my head against the wall and gave me BRAIN damage and that's why I'm in this chair. I can only really use my left arm, which sucks because I'm right-handed. So I lit the bedsheets on fire. That was the fourth time I ended up in the psych ward."

"You lit the bedsheets on fire?" Pedro slaps his leg, laughing.

1. DEVELOP A SUPPORT SYSTEM.

"Yes I did and I got away with it by proving to the court I couldn't use a lighter with my left hand." Susanna's dark gums peek out from the roots of her teeth.

The ruckus dies down as Charlie speaks up from behind his navy-blue snowman eyes. He doesn't look at Amelia. "This is my second time. I went to this really fancy private place the first time, where they gave us colonics and we had yoga twice a day. When I got out, my parents were like, 'Just so you know, that cost us $30,000,' and I'm like, WHY WOULD YOU TELL ME THAT? And they resented it." Charlie oozes privilege from his subtly shaped eyebrows down to his designer house slippers. "So the next time it got bad, they figured they'd throw me in here. 'Save money

AND save your life,' is what my mom said."

"That sucks."

2. . . . .

Amelia's mind is blank. I still can't think of anything. Charlie's eyelids are bruised. He's been purging again.

"They just want me to take pills. They think that a pill will solve all my problems. Pills don't automatically make your life better, do they, Marvin?"

"Pretty much, yeah." Marvin pauses, then corrects himself, "For someone like me. For someone like you, they're meant to help you temporarily deal with your problems because you're not distracted by the mess in your head. But my brain is much different from yours, I'll have to take mine for the rest of my life." For the rest of my life. "What are they giving you?"

Before Charlie can answer, Rosemary throws open the door and yells down the hallway, "I HAVE TO WASH MY VAGINA!"

"We're tired of hearing about it you fucking slut!" complains Maxwell.

"IT'S ITCHY!"

"No one—"

"I need to WASH it—"

"Gives a shit—"

"Help me wash it!"

"About your disease-ridden—"

"I NEED TO WASH IT!"

"—cumhole!"

An orderly leads Rosemary out of the lounge, and some of their rare good cheer goes with her.

Pedro looks up from the floor, his voice heavy with shame. "I don't even know how many times I've been admitted. I don't remember all of them. But the first time was for beating up my parents in the middle of the night. I just couldn't take it anymore. The plotting and the scheming. Pretending to be asleep but they wanted me DEAD! They were PLOTTING!"

Marvin puts a hand on the young man's chest, transferring his calm demeanor to the boy. "Calm down, man, you're with friends."

Help them.

Pedro takes a drag of his cigarette and exhales through his nose.

2. HELP THEM.

"Thanks. I just get carried away sometimes."

"We all do." Help us.

"Well I never want to end up here again," Amelia adds to the confessions collecting in the middle of the room. "It smells like piss. I'll use a gun next time."

Charlie finally looks at Amelia, with wounded shock. "I thought you weren't suicidal anymore."

"Not at this minute. But when it comes back, as it always does, then I'll know to go for efficacy and not worry about the mess." They all look at Amelia, who is as casual about death as they are about their own stories. She does not understand the sudden tension in the room. "What?" Their disapproval smells like expired Tempera paint.

Charlie stands up and moves his eyes rapidly between Amelia's innocent face and the wall next to her head.

"I don't think you should do it. Even when that moment comes," he says.

"What a loss."

"So stupid."

"Hey, fuck you guys!" Susanna comes to her defense. "You don't know what it's like to wanna die all the time! It's like being burned at the stake! So back off because it's her decision. Right, Amelia?"

"Hell yes." The sounds of the room are ringing in her ears. Inhale. Exhale. Wheezing. Phlegm tickling its way up the esophagus. The exhaust system. Dirty filters. Up there, and in here—IN the lungs.

Charlie aims his hostility at Amelia. "So . . . are you gonna play again or not?"

"Yeah, actually," she says defensively. "Dr. Stephens is bringing in some sheet music. He said I could play from four to four thirty every weekday."

"Awesome!" Marvin smiles, as Susanna adds, "Fuck yeah!"

"Wait now, I don't know if anyone else is allowed to be in there." I want to do it alone. I want to be alone.

"How are they gonna keep everyone out? Take down ALL of us?" laughs Pedro. "You saw how it was, even Lucia was quiet! It was like a spell."

Amelia deflects the projection, "Well it was Marvin's idea."

"Marvin?"

"Yeah, he said if I missed music so much it might be good for me to play some. And he picked the lock."

"Guilty," Marvin smiles proudly.

Charlie knuckles his bony shoulder, and gives his gratitude to Marvin instead. "Marvin, you are a genius. That's the first real music I've heard in almost a month. It was like . . . rejoining. Just . . . fucking spectacular."

I want to be alone! Amelia yells in her head, but chooses more careful words. "No offense, Charlie, but it's not for you. It's not for any of you; it is entirely selfish. I am desperate in this noise and silence without music, and I need it. Sorry."

"Well," says Susanna, flipping her stringy hair hard enough to snap her fragile vertebrae, "no offense, Amelia, but we don't give a fuck WHY you're doing it."

"We all benefit from your selfishness," adds Marvin.

Amelia sighs. I don't want to share this with you. Please just leave me alone, just leave me alone, just *LEAVE ME ALONE!*

"Fine. You can come listen."

THE PROPHECY

Amelia doesn't knock. Charlie is face down on the bed, weeping into the real sheets she could hang herself with, thin as a skeleton in a coffin. She kneels on the hard, grey linoleum next to his head and speaks softly. "Charlie?" He lifts his face and looks at her, eyes black with despair. Amelia touches the space between with her fingertips and says, "What's going on?"

Charlie smashes his face back into the pillow and moans, "They're putting me on the transdermal morphine patch."

"What the fuck?" What does that mean? "What does that mean?"

"It means I'm going to get fat!" he suddenly screams into her face. His terror is palpable. Amelia touches his shoulder blade through his shirt, petting his hemorrhaging little wing stump. The words come out of him like bile. "It means I'm hopeless, Amelia." His stripped esophagus rattles when he talks. "It means the only thing left is to drug me into oblivion and get me so fucked up that I don't care what goes in my mouth." He is bound by his knotted muscles. "I'm gonna get fat. They're going to turn me into a pig and there's nothing I can do." He lays his head back onto the pillow, facing her, tears running freely.

"Charlie, you can refuse treatment. It's your right as a patient. They can find some other way, some other medicine—"

"What other medicine? An antidepressant? I've tried every one!" He rubs his wet, bloodshot eyes, pink as pork. "Xanax? I eat but purge when it wears off. This is the last resort."

"There has to be something . . ." Amelia clutches at ideas.

"I've tried it!" Charlie spits, standing. He grabs the thin layer of skin on his abdomen and squishes it together. "Look at this shit! I'm disgusting, I'm FUCKING DISGUSTING!" he cries. Salt water runs down his face. Spittle forms at the corners of his mouth and he groans, "I'm going to be fat. And no one's ever going to love me ever."

Then Charlie breaks down.

::SILENCE::

Amelia gingerly touches his elbow and he jerks away. "Charlie—"

"I see it now. I see it. I'M the freak, Amelia." His eyes harden as he straightens his torso. "I'm the freak. And they're going to take my whole life away from me. This patch is going to ruin my life."

"You can go to one of those treatment centers for eating disorders," she attempts.

"Like the one my parents sent me to last time? The one that cost them $30,000? The one that they resented and punished me for?" He crosses his arms over his wet baby bird chest. "I told you what they're like."

::SILENCE::

"You're only a freak because you're killing yourself, too," Amelia whispers. "Can't you see that?" She bites the inside of her lips to briefly experience the comforting feeling of feeling. He allows her to touch his jaw with the back of her hand, as one would do with a strange dog. "I think we should still talk after we get out." Amelia opens her hand and turns the palm toward his smooth skin. "I think . . ." She thinks. "I think we need each other."

The bridge of Charlie's nose contracts into a triangle. He looks across the room at the pine dresser she can hang herself on, shakes his head, and exhales through his nose. "Amelia." The air grows still. "You're never gonna see me again." He looks over his pointy cheekbones and into her strange eyes. "And if you do, I'll be unrecognizable."

The room purrs with the frequency of the metal pipes in the walls. Rejected, Amelia looks at the shatterproof glass in the window behind him, willing it to explode and shred her to pieces.

::SILENCE::

She dismisses herself without another word.

THE LAST SUPPER

Amelia avoids the dry pork chop on her tray, talking around a mouthful of crispy green beans that taste like dark, rich soil.

"Looks like Monday." Susanna loads a quarter of her vegetables onto Amelia's plate, who swallows only half the food in her mouth before continuing, "Then a week to pack, then off to that fucking hellhole."

"What? You don't like your parents? Your dad seems like a good guy," observes Charlie.

"I love my family. I hate Florida."

"Why?"

Amelia stops eating long enough to give a short list: "The heat, the rednecks, the old people, the Yankees, gators, water moccasins, flying cockroaches."

Susanna squeals.

"Yeah, and they're like this big." Amelia uses both hands to illustrate the size of a Palmetto bug. "Disney, tourists, the stink of the marsh, hurricanes—the list goes on and on." She steals one of Susanna's fries and pops it in her mouth, savoring the salt. "Once, it got so hot that my rearview mirror melted off my windshield."

"Yes, but at least it's not ten degrees all winter," says Marvin.

Amelia sneaks a halved pear off Susanna's tray, and says, "BUT, if it doesn't freeze at all, we have twice as many mosquitos." She spears the entire thing with her spork, and lifts the fruit to her mouth. Unbleached linen. Sheets drying on a line in the summer sun. Stealing pears from her next-door neighbor and trying to sell them to the postman in the front yard. The flesh has the consistency of a thick wool blanket. It squishes between her teeth. Sensory bliss for her brain.

Charlie gives in and takes a bite of fruit. His mood hangs in his eyes like sharp icicles.

The pear's nutty, light taste occupies Amelia's attention, until Marvin says, "We'll miss you." The corners of his eyes crinkle up with laugh lines, but his smile is muted. Amelia stops eating.

Pedro looks up from his plate. "Yeah, me, too."

"I'm gonna need to find another garbage disposal for my food," says Susanna as she transfers a quarter of her fries to Amelia's plate. "Back to hiding it in my pockets, I guess." She smiles her rotting grin. Charlie's expression is unfathomable. He says nothing.

"I'll miss you, too, my insane cohorts. But it's back to Daseinland for me." Only Marvin gets the joke. "What about you guys? Any of you get a timeline yet?"

Susanna rolls her yellow eyes, but Pedro looks hopeful. "I'm getting out next week, too. The new medication is working good," he says. "And once I'm out, I'll know to keep the lights on at night." He playfully nudges Amelia with his elbow. "And I'll know that I like Beethoven."

"They're saying three days after I start the patch," says Charlie, nibbling at the pear. He looks Amelia in the eye. Human. "I guess we'll see. I mean, what's the worst that could happen? I get really high." She appreciates his attempt at positivity.

They all look at Marvin, who rubs his forehead with one hand and takes off his glasses. "I feel worse," he says. Marvin pinches his eyes shut with his forefinger and thumb, and crosses his other arm over his waist. "The depression is getting . . . really bad," he says with eyes closed.

What do I say? It will be over soon? It's just a phase? Don't be selfish? Pray about it? Amelia has no idea how to comfort him.

Susanna, of all people, steps in. "Marvin, you have the best chance out of all of us. You were smart enough to put yourself in here for exactly this reason. Meds have worked for you before, you'll balance out. That don't make it easier, but at least you know you can be normal."

He opens his eyes, and gives a soft, humorless, "Ha."

Amelia's plate is as empty as her mind. The stringy pork sits awkwardly in the middle like a greasy heart.

There is only one thought: normal.

THE DOCTRINE
OF STEPHENS

In the hard chair in the ice-blue office, Amelia is listening to Dr. Stephens talk around decades of coffee stains. He considerately took the batteries out of the clock prior to her arrival. "I'm not completely comfortable with you leaving while still experiencing death ideation, but if you're not a danger to yourself or others I won't keep you here. Dr. Patel is an experienced psychiatrist and physician. He's well-respected at the Mayo Clinic, and I know he will be able to help you have a normal life."

Normal. The standard exchange begins in her head, *Nobody is normal* · · · Fuck you. I know exactly what normal means.

"Replace the bandages as needed, and don't take out any of your stitches. It will leave ugly scars that you'll regret once you are healthy."

Normal means not wanting to cut your eyes out or seeing maggots everywhere or praying to be murdered.

Amelia looks at the gauze neatly tucked into the crook of her elbow. I might as well walk out of here in a safety gown. *Shoulda got a gun.* Daddy. Andrew. Alexis. Mom · · · She screamed. "I'm nervous about seeing my friends and family." She screamed. "What should I expect? Am I supposed to tell people? Keep it a secret?"

"Suicide usually causes . . ." His molars connect and pull in his cheeks before he completes the thought, "Complicated family dynamics. There will be a lot of blame, and guilt, and anger. So be prepared for that." *SINNER!*

"I fucking hate being alive right now, and they're going to make it about them." *FAILURE!*

"They can't help it. Nothing makes a person feel more power-less than the suicide of a loved one. I've seen it with other patients, and that's why I'm warning you now." She screamed. "But as time goes on and your treatment gets more effective, those relation-ships will heal. Just like your scars." He gives her a pointed look. "Unless you pull your stitches out." He sits straight in his chair. "Keep a regular sleeping and eating schedule. Don't use alcohol or drugs. Exercise five times a week. Don't engage in behaviors that are self-destructive, and always take your medicine at exactly the same time of day, every day. That's the most important piece of advice I can give you: TAKE YOUR MEDS. If you're feeling better, it's because they're working, not because you don't need them anymore. Do not miss doses. Do not micromanage. Do not make changes in your regimen without consulting your psychiatrist."

::SILENCE::

"So that's your advice? Take your pills?"

"Every dose. Every day. Every SINGLE day," he commands. "That's your responsibility now. I told you once that you were not responsible for your illness, well, now you are. Are you up for that?"

Amelia blinks in terror. She is suddenly faced with having to plan a future. Her pupils contract in panic. Breathe. Breathe. Her impending lifetime seems to stretch into eternity. How am I going to live that long? How am I going to survive? "You really think I can be normal?"

"I think you can be better than normal, I think you can be yourself. I think you can be a free and independent human being."

Normal. "What if a pill doesn't work, or stops working?" Her heart flutters in her chest.

"If you're not noticing a positive change within two weeks, contact your doctor. You must maintain open lines of communication with him about what is working and what is not. We can't read your mind. If something isn't helping, you have to tell us so that we don't waste time with you feeling just functional."

"What's wrong with functional? I would definitely settle for functional."

"It's a low level of survival. You can feel good and be WELL."

Amelia's skepticism skirts across her lips. "Simply not wanting to kill myself all the time is good enough. Don't get my hopes up."

He sighs. "I realize that you've stopped believing in it, but know that we want you to take joy in life. Not to be artificially happy, but to find your authentic self, without your neurotransmitters handicapping you."

Taking four pills a day isn't artificial? "I don't know how to believe that."

"You will." The doctor confidently leans back, his hands behind his head. The chair skreels. "You've seen for yourself how much of a difference it makes just to sleep and eat on a schedule. If you stick with the program, communicate with your doctor, and take your pills EXACTLY as prescribed, you will."

If it doesn't work, I can always just blow my head off. "Okay. I'll give it a shot." She congratulates herself on the pun.

"And I want you to keep playing the piano. It will help the nerves in your mind and your forearms."

She thinks of the antique Winter upright waiting for her in Florida. The silence. I'll be living in silence. "What if I can't stand being separated from music like this? Is there any way for me to have the music, but lose the crazy shit?"

"No. I'm sorry," he apologizes. "Actually, I'm a little surprised you would even want that. Wasn't the constant music one of your most inconvenient symptoms?" ::SILENCE:: "Just keep playing and you'll get used to having control over it. Your capacity for creativity hasn't disappeared. Just transformed."

"And the constant noise?"

"Get yourself an iPod."

"That's a good idea." There is a moment of silent understanding between them.

Dr. Stephens stands and shakes Amelia's hand. "It was nice knowing you, Amelia."

"You, too. Thank you for . . . for everything," she says.

"Good luck."

PRACTICAL BLASPHEMY

"Let us pray." Amelia looks at the gaudy Easter decorations in distaste while Nurse Jessica prays. "Father, thank You for another day of Your blessings and mercy." Charlie, Susanna, and John Doe's eyes are open, too, but they don't look at each other. "We submit to Your Word and mighty power, and beg Your forgiveness for our many sins." This is bullshit. She brings it up at the beginning of every fucking session. "May You grant us healing through Your Son, Christ Jesus, who protects us now unto the end of time. Amen." I'm going to say something. "I know it's been a long week for many of you, so we're not doing anything taxing today. Amelia leaves tomorrow, and I think we should all thank her for the music she's been playing for us."

For us. Everybody's clown.

A few patients murmur their gratitude. The nurse claps her hands. "We will all get a chance to talk about songs that get us through hard times, after Amelia shares any last words she has for the group."

Amelia knows the routine—why you came in, how long you were here, what you learned, your plans for the future. It usually takes up half the session. She looks around at the bored faces. "I came in for trying to kill myself. I've been here for three weeks. I learned that religion is indistinguishable from insanity. I plan to get a degree in music therapy."

Nurse Jessica blinks her huge eyes at Amelia's curt response. "Would you care to elaborate?"

"From now on, I only believe in reality."

"And what is your definition of reality?"

"Facts agreed upon by multiple, independent, objective observers." Amelia has been obsessed for days with finding a suitable description of the concept. "I can't spend any more time wondering what is and isn't real. No one is torturing me or punishing me. I am free to make my own choices and live by my own rules, and I'm sick of all this bowing, scraping, posturing bullshit. God is probably not real. Or only as real as the pantheon before him. But it doesn't matter. It's irrelevant."

"You are a hopeless person," Rosemary scoffs.

Amelia looks straight into her ancient face. "I am. I AM hopeless, but it has nothing to do with religion. I just think it's better to face facts and accept chaos than to think our suffering is part of some special plan. Look at Pedro: he believes he will be healed. Wouldn't it be healthier to believe in his psychiatrist and the medication he's taking? Better to talk to his doctor instead of his priest? No god is going to help him."

"That's blasphemy," croaks Rosemary.

"It's practical," counters Amelia. "Better than being a backwards, racist, Pharisee whore like you. I could quote you ten Bible verses right now that would shame you out of your chair."

"Whoa! Girl fight!" yells Maxwell.

Nurse Jessica tries to steer the conversation to a smoother course. "And there's the key word: shame. Does anyone know the difference between guilt and shame?" The patients watching Amelia and Rosemary only need popcorn. "Guilt is about what you DO. Shame is about who you ARE," she tries.

Amelia shrugs and says, "Well, she IS a whore."

"Oh shit!" laughs Maxwell.

Nurse Jessica shushes him before turning back to Amelia.

"And you ARE being disrespectful. Is this how you want to waste your final group session? Insulting everyone?"

Amelia looks around the room and shrugs again. "I LIKE these people. Know how I used to fight with Lucia all the time? Yesterday, she turned pages for me while I played Chopin. I didn't know she could read music." Lucia looks confused by the words she doesn't understand, so Amelia cranes around to look at her and mimics playing the piano. She points at Lucia, and mimes turning pages. Lucia nods and smiles enthusiastically. "See? Obviously the four of them are my friends," she gestures to Charlie, Pedro, Marvin, and Susanna, "but now I know that Juanita likes Mozart's 'Requiem,' and Maxwell is a tenor, and John Doe cries when I play Ravel." She looks down at her socks. "That's what makes me want to study music therapy."

Nurse Jessica presses her lips together in disapproval, then says, "I'm not sure about your ability to work in the mental health field, but I think it's very good that you have long-term goals. What I'm hearing you say is that you're finding it easier to form connections now that you're making music outside of yourself."

"Exactly," Amelia agrees. "As much as I hate the silence, I'm more present. I may stick around out of sheer curiosity. We are this rare, insignificant, beautiful accident hurtling out in space with no one to care for us but ourselves. I'm choosing to embrace that chaos. If everything is absurd, the logical choice is suicide. But life is not logical. So, to truly be a participant in this absurdity, I must continue to live in spite of it."

"Some of those things are very good to hear," Nurse Jessica says with a generous smile. "Will you start the group discussion with song lyrics that got you through a hard time? Since your playing is the inspiration for our topic today? Just one," she winks like an idiot.

"The song doesn't have lyrics."

"Well, maybe you can play it for everyone before you leave tomorrow," she suggests.

Amelia nods, grateful for the song on a 2002 mixtape from an unrequited love. "I will." She wiggles her fingers and says, "And I'm sorry if I . . . if I insulted anyone or anyone's beliefs. I just had to work things out for myself."

After a second thought she amends, "Except for Rosemary. She's a fucking ignorant, racist whore."

2ND APOSTLES

Amelia stares blankly at a split in the wallpaper of the common room while her father and friends discuss her as if she's not there. *FAILURE.*

Noah speaks from his hooked nose. "So she'll be released, but only on the condition that she goes to Florida and lives with you." *FAILURE.*

Her father's eyes are animated. *FAILURE.* "Yes, and they've recommended a psychiatrist with the Mayo Clinic. He specializes in this different type of bipolar. He's supposed to be very good. What's his name again?" he asks Amelia.

They turn to her and her absent affect. The silence gets her attention.

There it is again—that look of expectation.

Unsure of what she is being asked, she throws out, "Whenever you guys want."

It is immediately clear that this is not the correct response. Wretched looks of disgusting sympathy crawl onto their faces.

Everybody's clown.

Constance's round eyes spark with relief, and she ends the awkwardness. "Oh yeah, I brought you these!" She extends her long arms toward the floor, digs in a fashionable striped bag, and gives Amelia a small bundle. Amelia takes it and unfolds a pair of sensible navy-blue dress socks that smell like Tupperware. The lab-created fabric is pleasantly slippery between her fingers.

"You got me socks?"

"Kind of," Constance says, taking them back. "See?" She holds them out to Amelia. "I cut the toes off and put a hole in for your thumb. So you can cover your bandages when you're out in public." *FAILURE.*

"That's . . . great." The socks are perfect. Clothes. "That's actually really awesome, thank you."

"Of course, you can't have them till you're out," she says, putting them back into her bag, "So I'll have them back at the apartment waiting for you. Four o'clock, right?"

Amelia takes a deep breath in. *FAILURE.* "More like four thirty. They want me to play one last time."

"I'm meeting her in the parking lot, then we'll drive back to the apartment," Amelia's father elaborates.

Constance continues her abject cheer. "Can we do anything to help?"

"Would you be up for making dinner?" asks her father.

"Absolutely!" she jumps at the chance. "Chicken okay?"

"Chicken is fine." Their voices are strained.

"I brought over some movies if—" Noah begins, but Amelia holds up her hand and stops him.

"Thanks guys, you're really wonderful, I just . . . I just want to be alone with my dad."

::SILENCE::

Noah rises, all elbows and knees. "That's cool."

"That's totally cool," says Constance, gathering her stuff. "We can just—"

"Not now, when I get home!" Amelia makes small gestures to their chairs, unwilling to accidentally expose the gruesome stitches at her elbows. "Please. Like I would ask you to leave. You're good friends. Thank you for coming to see me here." *FAILURE.*

There is a brief pause, before Constance's voice lowers to her normal, alto level of enthusiasm. "It's just . . . you were talking about it so much, and I didn't know when to start taking it seriously. Like, at what point does it go from a sarcastic joke to a cry for help?" She turns to Amelia's father. "I'm sorry we didn't stop her. I didn't think she would do it."

"Constance," Amelia interrupts her apology, "I waited until you were out of town on purpose. You, Chris, Jeremy . . . only Eli was left, and he was at work. If I could have, I would have done it in secret, but someone had to take care of Blue. I would have been happy if I'd disappeared from existence and been wiped from everyone's memories." Constance looks down at the grubby tabletop. "No one could have stopped me."

The only thing that could stop me is the sick, twisted genius who designed this entire ward and literally thought of EVERY WAY to kill yourself . . . then built the opposite. Safe as a playpen.

"Well, there were signs—" Noah's gentle vocal chords tighten in his larynx. "—and I ignored them. Coming here is the least I can do to make that up to you." *FAILURE.*

The guilt is crushing. "You don't owe me anything, Noah." She takes in his apologetic countenance, then looks to her friend cloaked in her cashmere bubble wrap. "Or you, Constance, or Dad." Daddy. "I'm willing to give this doctor and this medicine a chance." *FAILURE.*

Constance resumes her chirpy enthusiasm. It sticks in her teeth as she speaks. "At least it can't be any worse than the past ten years."

" . . . True." Amelia tries very hard to appreciate her efforts. "Always the optimist."

"Where's Charlie? I want to say bye to him, too." Amelia's father looks around the room.

"Probably sleeping in. He started his new medication last night, and they usually give you some time to adjust." She thinks of the days she spent on the floor of the shower, before recognizing the blue blur of his flannel pajama pants. "Oh, there he is!" Amelia waves at Charlie, who is partially dressed and walks as if he's carrying a two hundred pound sack on top of him. He slowly comes into focus, then slams into the seat at her table, disoriented. Amelia touches the edges of his clavicle and examines the event horizon of his pupils. "Dude . . . where are YOU right now?"

Charlie pitches to the left and points to his chest. "I'm just started . . . the night at night and I slept SO good, Amelia. I slept SO good."

She places her hands on each side of his face, and tries to make eye contact while his eyelids flutter. "Charlie, look. These are my friends Constance and Noah. Constance is one of my roommates, and Noah and I went to high school together. They're good people." Charlie shakes his head with his mouth open, a cavern of destruction.

Amelia's father gets his attention. "We just finished up a round of spades. What do you want to play?"

"Billyjabbit?" Charlie answers.

"How about gin?" her father suggests, and starts dealing the cards. His TMJ clicks as he grinds his teeth in concern. Keeping his cornflower eyes on the cards, he speaks to the table. "Thank you all for being such good friends to my daughter. And Charlie, I'm glad she had you while she was in here."

Charlie's eyes go average with shock. He turns his whole body toward Amelia. "Are you . . . are you are you getting out?"

"Yes, I told you that." She looks into his Cookie Monster eyes, googly and unfocused. "Are you alright?"

"Sorry, I'm just there and then at the . . . it's . . ."

Everyone is embarrassed for him.

"Wake up, Charlie!" Amelia claps her hands in front of his face. He struggles to open his eyes, then falls asleep sitting up. Their embarrassment turns to fear. Drool creeps out of the corner of his mouth.

Noah stands up. "Is he okay?"

"He could be having a seizure," worries Constance.

Amelia's father speaks from years of experience with drunkards and druggies, "No, he's just zonked out. Is he on some kind of opiate?"

"Daniel!" Amelia waves over the orderly. He jogs from the nurses' station.

"What's going on?"

"He's dead asleep," Amelia says. "Sitting up like that. Mid-sentence. Is something wrong with his meds?" Concern calcifies in her like layers of soap scum. Unrecognizable.

Daniel checks Charlie's vitals, and reassures everyone. "Nah, he's just sleepy. I'll get him back to his bed." He lifts Charlie in a fireman carry. "Come on, buddy. Let's get you back in bed so you can sleep this off."

They play the game in silence, with Charlie's unused hand screaming from his seat at the table.

THE BOOK OF ELLIOTT

Art therapy has just ended, and everyone gathers in an orderly ring around the piano. The pregnant therapist unlocks it with excitement, as silence settles over the room. Amelia lifts the bench so that it does not make a noise, and carefully places it eighteen inches away from the keyboard. The song comes to her without effort: "Bye," written and performed on a tragically out-of-tune piano by the late, great Elliott Smith. She plays from memory.

Her fingers comfortably start the **G minor** arpeggio. Dolente. Her left hand begins a downward slope: Root-Chord, Root-Chord. Her body sways with the 6/8 time signature. It is a sea of sound that rocks her neurons to sleep. The chord structure draws the venom from her wounds and blisters the keys. The rhythm is as constant as the tides. It dips into a well of emptiness and comes out dry. She is so thirsty.

Muscle memory carries her to the octaves. The tendons in her forearms feel flexible; her fingers dexterous. Rocking side to side with the triplets, Amelia follows the song down. Her left hand continues to alternate between root and chord, sentito. The melody moves upward from the **G**, courting sharps like hypodermic needles. Triste. 8va. The octaves return, and she revels in her plasticene scar tissue. She absorbs Elliott Smith's ruined chest and bloody hands through the keys. Accidentals appear in the melody like unwanted but brilliant thoughts. It is the perfect song for a sad, drunken clown, rolling back and forth in mock stupor.

The song walks downwards, wavering in expression but a

tempo. As her wrists get closer together, Amelia keeps time over heavy pedal. 1–2, 1–2. She is the prodigal son. She is Elliott's mother, screaming. She is stabbing herself in the chest, twice, just to make sure. Deeper and deeper she goes into the empty well. At the bottom is mud and she nurses the filth for every last drop. The last few notes are deep and doloroso, then an acciaccato glissando.

::SILENCE::

Amelia stands up. The group is quiet, expecting more.

Everybody's clown.

"I'm leaving now."

Maxwell is the first to come out of his reverie and understand her words. "Well, freak, this—" He approaches her, and lays a hand on her right arm. "—is an Indian burn." He wrenches her arm and does the Daffy Duck dance on his way out the door.

Charlie stumbles to hug her, still acclimating to his new meds. His clumsiness is repulsive. "You look beautiful in that shirt. I want you to keep it."

Amelia forces herself to smile, despite her disgust. He was right. "I will, Charlie. Thank you."

Susanna wheels herself forward and slips Amelia a nearly empty matchbook. "These are the matches I blamed on Rosemary," she whispers. "Use them well." *BURN US ALL.*

"You're my girl," says Amelia, palming the matches. "Hey, I hope you die soon."

"You, too, Amelia." Susanna balances her giant head on top of her spine. "You, too."

Amelia hoists up the box of sheet music, her stitches straining, and pushes it into Daniel's arms. "Please thank Dr. Stephens for me."

"I will. Good luck."

When she turns to push in the piano bench, Juanita appears

in front of her. She makes apologetic and ecstatic faces that Amelia does not understand, then gives her a quarter. The mute tries to communicate with gestures: piano.

Thank God.

Piano · · · Me.

Juanita points to the quarter.

"I can't take this," Amelia's heart pulses and Juanita insists on pushing it into her hand, choking out broken air. Finally, Amelia accepts. "Thank you. I'm gonna frame this when I get home."

Think. Her. The woman points to Amelia's head, then to herself again: remember me.

Lucia barges in, rapidly speaking Spanish to the mute. She makes the sign of the cross over Amelia and gives a short blessing in Spanish. Then, for the first time, the woman makes eye contact with Amelia.

Speaking as though rehearsed, Lucia parrots a short, broken sentence. "You stop." She grabs Amelia's hands and lifts them to waist level with bony fingers. "You stop. You don't hurt." Amelia grasps the quarter tightly, wishing the woman would take her hands off her. "You don't hurt." Amelia starts to squirm.

Marvin saves the day, politely excusing himself while maneuvering his body between Amelia and the staring woman. He waits until Lucia tears her eyes away from Amelia, before surreptitiously placing something in her hand. "I thought you should have this . . ."

Amelia looks down. It's the 'missing' remote control. "Mo-ther-fucker!" She gives him a hearty hug. "Now who's going to cause all the havoc?"

"Just gonna have to get on with this," he says, shielding his sleeve from the rest of the room. He flashes a razorblade at her. *Cracking ice, a murder of crows rising from a white tree, the dark is rising · · · Kill it KILL IT!*

She looks over his shoulder at Rosemary, who flips the bird.

"Open the battery compartment when you get out of the building. Just something to remember us by," he whispers. She puts a hand on his opposite shoulder.

"I will. Thanks. Good luck."

Pedro lingers by the door. "Thank you. For everything," he says sadly, and then just hugs Amelia for a long time.

"I'll think of you every time I play Beethoven," she comforts him.

Amelia gives Charlie one last look. He is too fucked up to say any parting words, too far gone to say, "See? I told you so. Unrecognizable."

Elliott Smith is splattered all over the walls like the precious blood of a genius.

"Bye," she says. And all else was

::SILENCE::

GENESIS

Amelia steps out of the building into the chilly spring air. Chicago at its finest. The petrichor reminds her of yesterday's rain, and her Floridian childhood spent contemplating the SPRING GREEN label on the side of a crayon. RoseArt was for the poor kids. Daddy always made sure we donated Crayola, so they wouldn't be embarrassed.

She looks for the cherry red Saab 900S Turbo that Chris bought for her birthday, but her vision is so bad that she can only determine that there are no moving vehicles nearby. The wind is cold. Amelia stands in the shade of the hospital, shivering in Charlie's boxers and threadbare T-shirt unraveling at the seams. She looks at the quarter, then at the remote, and remembers what Marvin said. She opens the battery compartment. In it is a single cigarette. David Bowie skips into her head without an intro, and she follows his instructions without question:

She takes the cigarette.

Puts it in her mouth.

Pulls out the matches, then lights one, then cigarette.

The toxic smoke is calling. It lingers.

She won't forget.

Oh · · · I'm a rock and roll suicide.

ACKNOWLEDGMENTS

First, I would like to acknowledge those who are treatment-resistant, or have been unable to find a working medication regimen thus far. I have undergone many adjustments and endured more hospitalizations since the conclusion of this book. I wish you the best of luck in finding competent psychiatrists and access to the psychopharmaceuticals that will help you live a reasonably normal and fulfilling life.

I would like to thank my father, who told me I would write this.

I would like to thank Gabriel Levinson of ANTIBOOKCLUB, who encouraged me to transform *Practical Blasphemy* from a screenplay to a novel.

I would like to thank my husband, whose unconditional love saves my life every day.

Special thanks to James Adams, Robert Cohn, and Caitlin Parrish—because when you feature people in your work, it is appropriate to give them recognition.

Thank you to my fellow patients, whose identities I have kept locked away to secure your privacy.

Also, thanks to those who visited me in the hospital who are not featured in this book, as well as friends and family who eventually forgave my suicide. I love you all, and am endlessly grateful for the support system you provide. I couldn't make it without you.

Dr. Satyen Madkaiker and Dr. Sricharan Moturi also deserve my gratitude. I don't know if you will ever fully comprehend what it is that you do for mentally ill people, but I hope you realize that you are in the business of saving lives. A thousand times thank you, thank you, thank you.

Last, but not least, thank you to every musician who has ever inspired, comforted, or tortured me. Dead or alive, you have left your mark.

PRACTICAL
BLASPHEMY

—

THE NEW TESTAMENT

LJT

ANTIBOOKCLUB

NEW YORK

Published in 2019 by ANTIBOOKCLUB

Design by Najeebah Al-Ghadban

ISBN 9780997592313 (paperback)

Library of Congress Control Number: 2019940401

Published in the United States of America

10 9 8 7 6 1 2 3 4 5